FINDING TRUE NORTH
CHANGING THE HABIT OF HOW WE VIEW GOD AND LIFE

DINO GRIFFIN

Finding True North

Paperback: ISBN: 9798993348506

This book is dedicated to my one true love,

Kristina Griffin

A Sail For The Winds Of God

CONTENTS

INTRODUCTION

"We are in danger of forgetting that we cannot do what God does, and that God will not do what we can do. We cannot save ourselves nor sanctify ourselves, God does that; but God will not give us good habits, He will not give us character, He will not make us walk aright. We have to do all that ourselves." Oswald Chambers

A s with any journey that we undertake, our approach can make the difference between a glorious ending or disastrous failure. Journeys require planning; the more difficult the road, the more important crucial the preparation.

One thing that every journey requires is a constant recalibration to determine where we are located in terms of our destination. This is even more true in a long journey.

Consider this. If you're traveling to a certain destination and you're off course by just one degree, then after one foot, you'll miss your target by 0.2 inches. That seems negligible. But after 100 yards, you'll be off by 5.2 feet. That seems small enough to be easily corrected. But after a mile, you'll be off by 92.2 feet. One degree is starting to make a difference. If you were trying to get from San Francisco to Washington, D.C., you'd end approximately 8 miles away. Here is where it gets interesting. Traveling the distance around the world, you would be around 69 miles off. In a rocket going to the moon, you'd be 663.5 miles off. Going to the sun, you'd miss by over 258,000 miles (nearly ten times the diameter of the earth). Traveling to the nearest star, you'd be off course by over 69 billion miles.

FINDING TRUE NORTH

Remember, that is just one degree off!

True north, also known as geographic north, is the direction along the Earth's surface towards the North Pole. It's a fixed point on the globe, unlike magnetic north, which changes based on the Earth's magnetic field.

There are several ways to find true north. A standard compass points towards magnetic north. To find true north, you need to adjust for the magnetic declination (at most places on the Earth's surface, the compass doesn't point exactly toward geographic north. The deviation of the compass from true north is an angle called "declination" or "magnetic declination"), of your location. The declination value for your area can be found from local maps or online resources.

In using the sun, in the northern hemisphere, if you face the sun at noon, you're facing approximately true south, thus your back will be towards true north. Alternatively, the shadow cast by a vertical object like a stick at noon will point towards true north.

If you are using the stars, in the northern hemisphere, you can find true north by locating Polaris, the North Star. Polaris is located nearly directly above the North Pole and serves as a reliable indicator of true north on clear nights.

Topographic maps and most online mapping services are oriented with true north at the top of the map. When using such a map, ensure that you align it correctly with your surroundings to determine true north.

So, with any journey, if you intend on reaching your destination you must first find true north, and secondly, you must check your travel against true north. If you use magnetic north as a reference point, you will miss your destination.

The question for a Christian is, what is our true north? There is only one answer to that question, but unfortunately in our society, there is much confusion and debate about how we get to our destination. It is mostly suggested that somehow, because we are so enlightened, we no longer believe there is any objective truth to be found so we must navigate by our feelings. This would be like determining our direction by magnetic north—it is ever changing according to the earth's changing magnetic field. In that same way, our societal magnetic north changes according to the social climate of our time.

We must return to our true north. True north, for the Christ follower, is the Word of God. It is the objective, reliable, and unchanging guide for our journey in this life. Many people start off their journey with God by following true north, but then get distracted by all the interference of magnetic north. Our so-called society of Christendom, in the United States, has even begun to question the validity of the Bible as our true north and are left with no real guidance in life.

The book you are now reading is intended as a "course correction" manual. That is not to say that the Bible is no longer true north. It is, in fact, just the opposite. Circumstances in America have led to such a distrust and speculative suspicion of the veracity of the Bible that I feel it is necessary to share this book as a pointer, or a more constant reminder, of the trustworthiness and need for Biblical thinking. We need this more than ever as believers around us seem morally and societally lost in a sea of relative truth.

This book contains ten declarative prayers designed to help you, as a believer, to build more Christlike character into your life. It is intended to produce in you a habitual way of thinking about Christ and your relationship to Him. The declarations are on one page and are followed by a single page that contains Scriptures which provide a biblical framework for the declarations.

It is suggested that you take one page of declarations per week. Read the declaration out loud at least twice a day. Then you should also set aside time to meditate on the scriptural portion of the declarations every day. This may sound monotonous or boring, but you are building into your life habits of thought that have not previously existed. For a full accounting on this type of prayer and meditation, I have included in the back of the book a small treatise on declarative prayer and meditation that I hope you will find helpful. It is designed to be a correction to the course you are on, making sure you are continually pointed toward the true north of the Scripture.

This is a book to keep on the shelf after you have gone through it once. Its design is to keep you on track. It is also a resource to turn to when you feel stuck in your Christian walk, or when you need some encouragement, or when you are simply worn out and don't feel like praying. Some people look at written prayer as "wrote", or "mechanical", or too insincere. But how can that be? The Bible (as I present it in the treatise in the back of the book) is full of prayers that have retained their substance, relevance and power over thousands of years. In fact, repetitive prayer can help in those times when you just feel burned out and spontaneous prayer doesn't work for you. It is a tool, not the thing itself, but it can be a helpful tool of remembrance and simply stating truth for your heart and soul to absorb.

In the second half of this book, I have included one hundred and forty daily readings. These are broader than just devotionals. Some are designed to lead you to prayer. Some are designed to lead you to meditation or reflection. And some are there to challenge your thinking concerning what you really believe is the truth of Scripture.

All in all, the preeminent goal of this book is to lead you to Jesus. The Word of God that I refer to is the Word of Jesus. The destination we long for and seek is to be with Jesus. I am not "in this" just so I will live eternally, I am in this because Jesus one day captured my heart and I want to live with Him, through Him, and because of Him. After all, the Scripture says that He alone is eternal life.

"We know also that the Son of God has come and has given us understanding, so that we may know Him who is true. And we are in Him who is true—even in Hi Son Jesus Christ. He is the true God and eternal life." 1 John 5:20 (NIV)

1

REPENTANCE DECLARATION

T oday I will live in repentance—turning from a life of self-determination to a life of following Jesus Christ. I confess my sins (be specific, ask God to reveal any sins you are not aware of) and ask You, Lord, to forgive me. I choose to see my sin through Your eyes, Lord, and embrace the pain of my choices. I will not minimize or cover over my sin and will seek godly sorrow over both my sin and its consequences. I accept responsibility for my sin and refuse to waste one more minute defending myself.

As I confess my sins, I am confident that God forgives me and also washes me clean. I affirm that God's kindness leads me to repent— His love calls to me and draws me even when I am far away. In His love, He has taken care of my sin on the cross. I can now stand clean before my Lord, the world and my own conscience. I free myself from any of shame and condemnation; knowing that even if my heart condemns me, God is greater than my heart (1 John 3:19-20).

I choose to live this day a life pleasing to God; walking by faith in complete obedience to the Holy Spirit. I expect much of myself today—determined to do nothing that is unworthy of the name of Christ. God is faithful to me; I will be faithful to Him. The sacrifice God desires is a broken spirit; I know that You will not reject a broken and repentant heart, O God (Psalms 51:17).

God has not given me a sinless life, but He has given me the ability, through confession and repentance, to make it right. I will keep a short account with God concerning my sin. When I sin, I will immediately turn from my sin and turn to God, confessing my sin and embracing the blessing of God's forgiveness through Jesus.

From this moment forward I will follow Jesus and seek to abide with Him at all times—at work and at play, through good circumstances and bad. I will remember who I am: a child of God purchased by Jesus' own blood.

I accept the responsibility for my past, but I choose to live looking forward. God's grace is always waiting for me in the future, so that even when I trip and fall, He is there to pick me up and set me on the path of living for His glory.

1

REPENTANCE AFFIRMATION

T he way into Christianity is the way on; we confess our sins and turn from our self-determination and follow Christ. It is a life-long process: we confess our sins, turn from them and turn toward God. I John 1:8-9 says, "If we claim we have no sin, we are only fooling ourselves and not living in the truth. But if we confess our sins to Him, He is faithful and just to forgive us our sins and to cleanse us from all wickedness."

So, there is no way around it, we still sin and we still periodically turn from following Jesus to go our own way. We fix this by owning up to our sins and going back to follow Jesus.

It is God's kindness that leads us to repent ("Or do you show contempt for the riches of His kindness, tolerance and patience, not realizing that God's kindness leads you toward repentance?" Romans 2:4 (NIV)) meaning that what He really wants is relationship with us—sin puts a distance between us that can only be mended by the cross.

If you cut a butterfly out of his cocoon, he will never fly; the struggle of breaking free from the cocoon produces the strength to fly. In that sense, Christians who have never known true repentance are like butterflies that have never flown; not having struggled against or resisted sin, they undergo an incomplete process of transformation.

Pain, real pain is a part of repentance. We see ourselves either through our own eyes: through our personal vanity, or through the eyes of divine love. The latter can be shattering, but it can change us forever if we will let it. False repentance is founded on selfishness: "Godly sorrow brings repentance that leads to salvation and leaves no regret, but worldly sorrow brings death." 2 Corinthians 7:10 (NIV) The truly repentant person just does not care who knows. The falsely repentant are always hedging their bet, always trying to cover up their own sinfulness. The falsely repentant accuse all those who are offended by their sin as "judging them." They are mostly concerned with themselves and excuses; trying to convince everyone that they have confessed their sin even while they try to minimize it.

However, discovering your sin is less important than discovering Christ. You cannot truly discover Christ without discovering at the same time what truly resides in your heart. But this is no time to save yourself; this is the time to die to yourself and live to God. "Then Jesus said to His disciples, 'If anyone would come after Me, he must deny himself and take up his cross and follow Me.'" Matthew 16:24 (NIV)

The following verse, although specifically addressed to the Nation of Israel, still applies to us today; God doesn't want sin in the way— doesn't want it to be our downfall. Through Christ, He has taken our sins away if we will but turn from them and turn toward Him. Today, and every day, God calls us to a life of repentance—it is the way we get in, and the way we go on.

"Therefore, O house of Israel, I will judge you, each one according to his ways, declares the Sovereign Lord. Repent! Turn away from all your offenses; then sin will not be your downfall. Rid yourselves of all the offenses you have committed, and get a new heart and a new spirit. Why will you die, O house of Israel? For I take no pleasure in the death of anyone, declares the Sovereign Lord. Repent and live!" Ezekiel 18:30 (NIV)

2

WHO I AM DECLARATION

From this moment forward I will live out of my identity of who God says I am. I will no longer identify myself by my sin or failure, or by my hurt. I am a saint of God. My name is written in the Lamb's book of life. I belong to God.

I will no longer be called the wounded one, or outcast, or lonely or afraid. Instead, I am confident in the Lord, full of joy, the overcoming one, the faithful one, the friend of God. I am the one who seeks the Lord's face.

I am raised with Christ and seated with Him in the heavenly realms. I am thankful to be called a child of God. I choose this day to rest in childlike wonder in the arms of my heavenly Father.

I have been rescued from the darkness of sin, self-hate and shame, and brought into the light of acceptance and love. I have total and instant access to God through the Holy Spirit who lives in me. And with the Holy Spirit's presence inside me, I am God's temple—a dwelling place of the living God.

I am reborn, and the evil one cannot harm me because God keeps me safe.

I am a new person—the old has passed and the new is yet to be experienced. I will not shrink back from life or circumstances; I will enter them with my eyes opened wide and my head up confident that the One that lives in me is greater than the devil who lives in the world.

I am a new person—and I will help create a new future by living as this new person for whom Christ gave His very life. I will no longer dwell in despair or self-pity or self-doubt; I will live courageously as a child of the King. I will no longer live as an imposter—saying that I believe in Christ but living as if He hardly exists.

I am established, anointed, and sealed by God and all my future is in His strong and capable hands. God's plan is for me to prosper and come to no harm—to give me hope and a future. I can do all things through Christ who gives me strength. I will smile and put a spring in my step today because God loves me!

2

WHO I AM AFFIRMATION

W hen you were born again, God placed your name in His Book of Life. Revelation 21:27 (NIV) says "Nothing impure will ever enter it, nor will anyone who does what is shameful or deceitful, but only those whose names are written in the Lamb's book of life." Your residence has changed; you became a citizen of Heaven.

You may have seen the film "Awakenings", which starred Robin Williams. The film is based upon the book with the same name, which was written by Dr. Oliver Sacks. Dr. Sacks recommended that his name be changed, and so the film follows a fictional Dr. Sayer through the summer of 1969 in the Bronx, New York. Dr. Sayer uses a new drug to try to treat some patients that appear to be catatonic, and for a time he is successful. However, patients who are treated with the drug develop a tolerance for it, and soon his patients return to their former state.

This is very similar to the lives of many Christians who have experienced only brief "awakenings" throughout their walk with Christ. Some go off to a conference or camp and rededicate their lives, only to slip back into the life of the uncommitted once back home. Others hear a great sermon and are moved, but only for a short time. They soon return to their old ways of thinking and relating.

This happens because their identity is still somehow with Adam, and not with Jesus. Those who have put their trust in Christ are no longer identified with Adam and by their sin, but with Jesus and His righteousness. Believers are no longer locked out of God's presence like Adam and Eve, they are seated with Christ in the heavenlies ("And God raised us up with Christ and seated us with Him in the heavenly realms in Christ Jesus." Ephesians 2:6 (NIV)) and are partners with all the saints: "giving thanks to the Father, who has qualified you to share in the inheritance of the saints in the Kingdom of light. For He has rescued us from the dominion of darkness and brought us into the Kingdom of the Son He loves." Colossians 1:12- 13 (NIV)

You are God's child: "Yet to all who received Him, to those who believed in His name, He gave the right to become children of God." John 1:12 (NIV)

You are Jesus' friend: "I no longer call you servants, because a servant does not know his master's business. Instead, I have called you friends, for everything that I learned from my Father I have made known to you." John 15:15 (NIV)

You have been justified: "Therefore, since we have been justified through faith, we have peace with God through our Lord Jesus Christ." Romans 5:1 (NIV)

You have access to God through the Holy Spirit: "For through Him we both have access to the Father by one Spirit." Ephesians 2:18 (NIV)

You are born of God, and the evil one cannot touch you: "We know that anyone born of God does not continue to sin; the one who was born of God keeps him safe, and the evil one cannot harm him." 1 John 5:18 (NIV)

You are God's temple; He lives in you by the Holy Spirit: "Don't you know that you yourselves are God's temple and that God's Spirit lives in you?" 1 Corinthians 3:16 (NIV)

You are established, anointed, and sealed by God and your future is in His hands: "Now it is God who makes both us and you stand firm in Christ. He anointed us, set His seal of ownership on us, and put His Spirit in our hearts as a deposit, guaranteeing what is to come." 2 Corinthians 1:21-22 (NIV)

3

PERSONAL RESPONSIBILITY DECLARATION

T oday I am taking responsibility for my past, my present and my future. I choose this moment to free myself from the bondage of my past and release myself into a greater and clearer future that I am responsible for.

I refuse to blame my parents, spouse, boss, friends, enemies, or especially God for my present circumstance. My level of education, my health or lack thereof, my genes, or even my circumstances will no longer affect my future in a negative way. I will lose the language of "give me a break" or "why me?" and choose to see my life as a result of my choices and not the whim of every circumstance that comes my way. I will become free; I will not let my history or circumstance control my destiny. I am responsible for my life.

I choose to treat other people the way I want to be treated; I will not allow others to dictate how I treat them. I will let no one control me by "making me angry"; I will choose to manage my emotions because I know that I will reap what I sow.

I am careful to control what I say, realizing that the tongue is very powerful to bless or to curse. My destiny is influenced by the words that I choose.

When I am tempted to ask, "why me?" I will choose to say, "why not me?" I will see challenges as opportunities to trust God, to learn and grow. Problems are an acceptable part of my life: I am in this moment either about to leave a problem, about to encounter one, or in the middle of one. Faced with any problem, I still have choices to make. I will make one. I will not put it off. God didn't put in me the ability to always make the correct choice, but He did give me the ability to choose and to make it right. My emotional state will not interfere with the course of my life. I'll stand behind my choices by God's grace. I will not live my life as an apology; I will not hide behind excuses.

Where I am today is a combination of my choices and my thinking. Today I will begin to change where I am by changing the way I think.

I am not a victim. I have the freedom to make the choices in life that lead to what God has called me to. I am not called to worry—I am called to act.

My thoughts will be constructive. I won't dwell on the past, and I won't constantly worry about my problems. I will think about the solutions of the future. I will choose to think about things that are true, noble, right, lovely, admirable, and worthy of praise. I am responsible for my own life.

3

PERSONAL RESPONSIBILITY AFFIRMATION

G od calls us to be responsible for our lives. He made this clear to the nation of Israel through the prophet Ezekiel: "As sure as I'm the living God, you're not going to repeat this saying in Israel any longer. Every soul—man, woman, child—belongs to Me, parent and child alike. You die for your own sin, not another's...The soul that sins is the soul that dies. The child does not share the guilt of the parent, nor the parent the guilt of the child. If you live upright and well, you get the credit; if you live a wicked life, you're guilty as charged." Ezekiel 18:3-4, 20 (MSG)

We cannot blame God or others for our sin: "When tempted, no one should say, 'God is tempting me.' For God cannot be tempted by evil, nor does He tempt anyone; but each one is tempted when, by his own evil desire, he is dragged away and enticed. Then, after desire has conceived, it gives birth to sin; and sin, when it is full-grown, gives birth to death." James 1:13-15 (NIV) We are responsible for our sin. If we don't say no in the enticement stage, we will reap full- blown sin and separation from God. There is no sin in temptation; sin comes when we entertain the temptation.

We reap what we sow; if we sow kindness and mercy, we will reap kindness and mercy. God expects us to treat everyone the way we want to be treated ourselves. "Do unto others as you would have them do unto you." Luke 6:31 (NIV) If we sow sin, we will reap spiritual death; we will be lethargic and weak in our relationship with Him and we will be less and less able to resist the enticement of sin. "Do not let sin control the way you live; do not give in to sinful desires." Romans 6:12 (NLT)

"Or take ships as an example. Although they are so large and are driven by strong winds, they are steered by a very small rudder wherever the pilot desires. Likewise, the tongue is a small part of the body, but it makes great boasts. Consider what a great forest is set on fire by a small spark. The tongue also is a fire, a world of evil among the parts of the body. It corrupts the whole person, sets the whole course of his life on fire, and is itself set on fire by hell." James 3:4-6 (NIV) If we control our tongue, we control our destiny. "On that day they will be told that they are either innocent or guilty because of the things they have said." Matthew 12:37 (CEV)

Many people think they can wait to get their lives straight with God, but God warns: "Let no debt remain outstanding, except the continuing debt to love one another, for he who loves his fellowman has fulfilled the law. The commandments ...are summed up in this one rule: 'Love your neighbor as yourself.' Love does no harm to its neighbor. Therefore, love is the fulfillment of the law. And do this, understanding the present time. The hour has come for you to wake up from your slumber, because our salvation is nearer now than when we first believed. The night is nearly over; the day is almost here. So let us put aside the deeds of darkness and put on the armor of light." Romans 13:8- 12 (NIV)

"Finally, brothers, whatever is true, whatever is noble, whatever is right, whatever is pure, whatever is lovely, whatever is admirable--if anything is excellent or praiseworthy--think about such things." Philippians 4:8 (NIV)

4

MOVING FORWARD DECLARATION

T oday I choose to move forward. I refuse from now on to remain at a standstill—when I am tempted to be immobilized by fear or when I am stuck in indecision, I will choose movement rather than passivity. I will be single-minded with the wisdom that comes from God. When faced with the possibility of doing something or nothing, I will seize the moment and always choose to act!

I refuse to be an emotional couch potato. I will resist the sin of laziness and will create a habit of movement. I will not be timid, but will act in the power, love and self-discipline that come from God. I will fan into flame the gifts that God has given me—I will expend my life rather than save it.

I will focus on the goal—keeping my eyes fixed on Jesus.

I will give God thanks for every day that I can draw breath. I will count my blessings and no longer be distracted by what might be wrong with my life. Today, I will move forward.

I will, like the Apostle Paul, fight the good fight and keep the faith. I will be courageous and bold.

I will inspire others with my activity, not drown them with my negativity. I am a leader; leaders are people of influence. I will move forward so that others can do the same. I will encourage others to move forward.

I will no longer be indecisive; I will make a decision. I will hear God as best I can, but will no longer stay in the valley of indecision because I can't hear Him perfectly. I will be daring and courageous. Fear will no longer dictate my life. For too long, fear has outweighed my desire to make things better for my family and for people around me. Never again! People will hardly recognize the new me! I have unmasked fear for the ghost that it is—a charlatan who never really had any power over me.

I will make my decisions quickly and change my mind slowly; rather than repeating the same sad pattern of making slow decisions and changing my mind quickly.

I will forget what is behind and strain toward what is ahead. I won't be afraid for God is always with me. I will move forward!

4

MOVING FORWARD AFFIRMATION

I any of you lacks wisdom, he should ask God, who gives generously to all without finding fault, and it will be given to him. But when he asks, he must believe and not doubt, because he who doubts is like a wave of the sea, blown and tossed by the wind. That man should not think he will receive anything from the Lord; he is a double-minded man, unstable in all he does." James 1:5-8 (NIV)

"For this reason, I remind you to fan into flame the gift of God, which is in you through the laying on of my hands. For God did not give us a spirit of timidity, but a spirit of power, of love and of self- discipline." 2 Timothy 1:6-7 (NIV)

"Let us fix our eyes on Jesus, the Author and Perfecter of our faith, who for the joy set before Him endured the cross, scorning its shame, and sat down at the right hand of the throne of God." Hebrews 12:2 (NIV)

"I have fought the good fight, I have finished the race, I have kept the faith. Now there is in store for me the crown of righteousness, which the Lord, the righteous Judge, will award to me on that day--and not only to me, but also to all who have longed for His appearing." 2 Timothy 4:7-8 (NIV)

"Be on your guard; stand firm in the faith; be men of courage; be strong." 1 Corinthians 16:13 (NIV)

"I want to know Christ and the power of His resurrection and the fellowship of sharing in His sufferings, becoming like Him in His death, and so, somehow, to attain to the resurrection from the dead. Not that I have already obtained all this, or have already been made perfect, but I press on to take hold of that for which Christ Jesus took hold of me. Brothers, I do not consider myself yet to have taken hold of it. But one thing I do: Forgetting what is behind and straining toward what is ahead, I press on toward the goal to win the prize for which God has called me heavenward in Christ Jesus." Philippians 3:10-14 (NIV)

"Be strong and courageous. Do not be afraid or terrified because of them, for the Lord your God goes with you; He will never leave you nor forsake you." Deuteronomy 31:6 (NIV)

5

AN UNDIVIDED HEART DECLARATION

I begin this journey of my life today with a first step. For too long I have been wishy-washy and uncertain, being pulled to the left and the right, taking two steps forward and three back. Today I will be of one heart and mind—wholly devoted to God and following His ways. No longer will I give my heart to the things of this world. No longer will I be more devoted to my own cause than to the Lord's. I will not walk in fear of mankind, or of the opinions of others, but I will only walk in the fear of the Lord.

Today I am charting my course. I will no longer nourish a hard heart and be insensitive to the voice of the Holy Spirit in my life. When the Lord speaks to me, I will unhesitatingly obey. I will not grieve the Holy Spirit by listening to all the clamoring voices of the world around me; I will give God my undivided attention.

I have a resolute heart. I will greet every new morning with an expectancy of the opportunities that God will send. I will no longer live to please myself or those around me; I will live with the single purpose of pleasing God. All my actions will be checked by this one great passion, "Is this pleasing to God?" I will serve God with all my heart, soul and mind.

I am not timid. I will turn from evil to follow God. I will not envy those who rebel against God—I will not covet their lives, experiences or possessions. I have been lured away from my devotion to God by watching the world around me. Instead, I will be zealous for the fear of the Lord. I will honor God by being content with what I have, confident that I can approach Him in boldness for all that I need.

I will not serve God and money. I will trust that God will provide for all my needs.

I will not allow circumstances to erode that trust. I will work hard and use my wealth wisely, always aware that God gives me the ability to gain wealth and all that I have belongs to Him.

My heart will no longer be divided. I have this one main passion: to love God with all my heart, and with all my soul, and with all my mind, and with all my strength. I will also love others as well as I love myself.

5

AN UNDIVIDED HEART AFFIRMATION

God wants us undivided in our devotion to Him. "Teach me Your way, O Lord, and I will walk in Your truth; give me an undivided heart, that I may fear Your name." Psalms 86:11 (NIV)

"I will give them an undivided heart and put a new spirit in them; I will remove from them their heart of stone and give them a heart of flesh." Ezekiel 11:19 (NIV)

An undivided heart is one that fears the Lord. "These were his instructions to them: 'You must always act in the fear of the Lord, with faithfulness and an undivided heart.'" 2 Chronicles 19:9 (NLT)

"I ripped the kingdom from the hands of David's family and gave it to you, but you weren't at all like My servant David who did what I told him and lived from his undivided heart, pleasing Me." 1 Kings 14:8 (MSG)

"And now, O Israel, what does the Lord your God ask of you but to fear the Lord your God, to walk in all His ways, to love Him, to serve the Lord your God with all your heart and with all your soul." Deuteronomy 10:12 (NIV)

"And he said to man, 'The fear of the Lord--that is wisdom, and to shun evil is understanding.'" Job 28:28 (NIV)

"The fear of the Lord is the beginning of wisdom; all who follow His precepts have good understanding. To Him belongs eternal praise." Psalms 111:10 (NIV)

"Do not let your heart envy sinners, but always be zealous for the fear of the Lord." Proverbs 23:17 (NIV)

From the beginning, God made it clear that He will not share His name with another, and there will be no gods beside Him. That is affirmed in the New Testament. "No one can serve two masters. Either he will hate the one and love the other, or he will be devoted to the one and despise the other. You cannot serve both God and money." Matthew 6:24 (NIV) You can either depend on your own strength in terms of wealth, or you can trust God. This doesn't mean we can excuse ourselves from hard work, it means that even our hard work it is God's hands that supply our need, not our own.

"And my God will meet all your needs according to His glorious riches in Christ Jesus." Philippians 4:19 (NIV)

God is always first and best in an undivided heart. "One of the teachers of the law came and heard them debating. Noticing that Jesus had given them a good answer, he asked Him, 'Of all the commandments, which is the most important?' 'The most important one,' answered Jesus, 'is this: "Hear, O Israel, the Lord our God, the Lord is one. Love the Lord your God with all your heart and with all your soul and with all your mind and with all your strength." The second is this: "Love your neighbor as yourself." There is no commandment greater than these.'" Mark 12:28-31 (NIV)

6

FORGIVING OTHERS DECLARATION

Today, in God's strength, I choose to forgive everyone who has ever wronged me. I will no longer hold on to the past, to the pain, or to the injustice I have received at the hands of others. I am not in the hands of any man or woman; I am in the hands of God.

I choose to walk in forgiveness today. This is an act of my will. Forgiveness is not a feeling; it is a choice. I will face any feelings of unforgiveness today with a choice to forgive. I will not keep a grudge. I will wish no ill-will to those who have wronged me. I can have firm boundaries with those who harm me yet still walk in forgiveness toward them.

When I am tempted to hold on to unforgiveness, I will remember that God through Christ has forgiven me. While I was still a sinner, before I had ever turned toward God, Christ died for me—for all my sins. I will forgive over and over again, not because people deserve forgiveness, but because I have been forgiven.

I choose to walk in forgiveness today knowing that unforgiveness damages my relationship with God. I will not walk in the lie that I can hold things against others and be okay with God. I know that as I forgive, I will be forgiven. I will forgive myself because not doing so says my sin is bigger than God's forgiveness.

I am a forgiving person. If my brother or sister sins, I will reprove them. If they repent, I will forgive them, even if they continue the cycle of sin and repentance. I will keep no record of wrongs.

I am a forgiving person. I understand that people are in process in their relationship with God, so I will be patient and compassionate toward others. I choose to love others even when their actions hurt me. I will bear with the faults of others and be slow to anger and quick to forgive.

I will walk in forgiveness today, even toward my Christian brothers and sisters who have hurt me and sinned against me. I will be kind and compassionate to them, choosing to forgive just as Jesus has forgiven me. I will not be a bitter, hurting and unforgiving person. I am free from the sins of others and I will no longer allow them to determine how I live. I am free to forgive and to love.

6

FORGIVING OTHERS AFFIRMATION

A s Christians, God holds us to a higher standard of forgiveness because we have been forgiven even when we did not deserve it. "'Forgive us our debts, as we also have forgiven our debtors. And lead us not into temptation, but deliver us from the evil one.' For if you forgive men when they sin against you, your heavenly Father will also forgive you. But if you do not forgive men their sins, your Father will not forgive your sins." Matthew 6:12-15 (NIV)

"But God demonstrates His own love for us in this: While we were still sinners, Christ died for us." Romans 5:8 (NIV)

"At that point Peter got up the nerve to ask, 'Master, how many times do I forgive a brother or sister who hurts me? Seven?' Jesus replied, 'Seven! Hardly. Try seventy times seven.'" Matthew 18:21-22 (MSG)

"Then the master called the servant in. 'You wicked servant,' he said, 'I canceled all that debt of yours because you begged me to. Shouldn't you have had mercy on your fellow servant just as I had on you?' In anger his master turned him over to the jailers to be tortured, until he should pay back all he owed. This is how my heavenly Father will treat each of you unless you forgive your brother from your heart." Matthew 18:32-35 (NIV)

We are called to rise above hypocrisy and be who we say we are, and to act as we are called to be. "And when you stand praying, if you hold anything against anyone, forgive him, so that your Father in Heaven may forgive you your sins." Mark 11:25 (NIV)

As we do, so will we be done by. "Do not judge, and you will not be judged. Do not condemn, and you will not be condemned. Forgive, and you will be forgiven." Luke 6:37 (NIV)

Paul writes to the Corinthians that love keeps no record of wrong. Jesus affirms this in the book of Luke. "So, watch yourselves. 'If your brother sins, rebuke him, and if he repents, forgive him. If he sins against you seven times in a day, and seven times comes back to you and says, "I repent," forgive him.' The apostles said to the Lord, 'Increase our faith!'" Luke 17:3-5 (NIV)

We are to be a people who act a certain way. The Bible puts "wheels on that" with particular instructions of what Christian behavior looks like. "Therefore, as God's chosen people, holy and dearly loved, clothe yourselves with compassion, kindness, humility, gentleness and patience. Bear with each other and forgive whatever grievances you may have against one another. Forgive as the Lord forgave you. And over all these virtues put on love, which binds them all together in perfect unity." Colossians 3:12-14 (NIV)

"Be kind and compassionate to one another, forgiving each other, just as in Christ God forgave you." Ephesians 4:32 (NIV)

7

ENDURANCE DECLARATION

S tarting right now, I choose to walk in the joy of the Lord. Few people have been able to grasp the truth of how powerful this attitude can be. Joy is not an emotional phantom that mysteriously shows up and just as quickly disappears from my life from time to time. Joy is a choice. It is not ignoring the pain or tragedy of life; it is simply not allowing the pain and tragedy of life to hold my life hostage to depression and a dark outlook. I will recount the goodness and blessing of God even as I face difficulties. Today, I choose joy.

I possess a grateful spirit. In the past I have been discouraged by my present circumstances until I compared those circumstances to those who are less fortunate. It is impossible for depression to take root in a thankful heart. God has given me many gifts, and for these I will be grateful. Too often I have come to God as a beggar, always asking for more and never thankful for what I have. I don't want to be seen as a grasping, self-centered and ungrateful child. I will go forward in thankfulness to defeat the powers of the devil.

Today, I choose to persist without exception. I will not give up, I will not give in. I will fix my eyes on Jesus. A sailor who focuses on the storm will lose his way; but one who focuses on the lighthouse will bring his ship safely home. I will remember all that Jesus went through on my behalf so that I will not grow weary or lose heart and quit. He didn't quit and neither will I.

The enemy's best work is to sometimes con us to use his means and ways. Today I refuse any alliance with the dark lord. I will walk in "an opposite spirit"; when I am cursed, I will bless, when I am hurt, I will show mercy, when I am persecuted, I will not quit. I can do all things through Christ who gives me strength.

I want to reign with Christ, so I will persevere and not give up. I will be faithful to God because He is faithful to me. I will see hardship and difficulty in my life as sandpaper—God using hardship to make me into the kind of special person He wants me to be. An athlete does not enjoy the pain of training, but enjoys the results of training.

I will watch my life and the principles that I live by closely; I will be diligent in keeping them sharp and truthful. I believe in the future that I cannot see. I will walk by faith and not fear. I will never give up!

7

ENDURANCE AFFIRMATION

T hen Nehemiah the governor, Ezra the priest and scribe, and the Levites who were instructing the people said to them all, 'This day is sacred to the Lord your God. Do not mourn or weep.' For all the people had been weeping as they listened to the words of the Law. Nehemiah said, 'Go and enjoy choice food and sweet drinks, and send some to those who have nothing prepared. This day is sacred to our Lord. Do not grieve, for the joy of the Lord is your strength.'" Nehemiah 8:9-10 (NIV)

There is real power in thanksgiving. Judah defeated the Moab and Ammon by sending worshipers ahead of the army giving thanks to God: "After consulting the people, Jehoshaphat appointed men to sing to the Lord and to praise Him for the splendor of His holiness as they went out at the head of the army, saying: 'Give thanks to the Lord, for His love endures forever.'" 2 Chronicles 20:21 (NIV)

There is no such thing as my "private religion" when it comes to Christianity. It is not only a "team sport," it is also out there for everyone to see, even those in Heaven. "Therefore, since we are surrounded by such a great cloud of witnesses, let us throw off everything that hinders and the sin that so easily entangles, and let us run with perseverance the race marked out for us. Let us fix our eyes on Jesus, the author and perfecter of our faith, who for the joy set before Him endured the cross, scorning its shame, and sat down at the right hand of the throne of God. Consider Him who endured such opposition from sinful men, so that you will not grow weary and lose heart." Hebrews 12:1-3 (NIV)

We are not called to just hang on; we are called to persevere while exhibiting the character of Christ. "We work hard with our own hands. When we are cursed, we bless; when we are persecuted, we endure it." 1 Corinthians 4:12 (NIV)

"Endure hardship with us like a good soldier of Christ Jesus." 2 Timothy 2:3 (NIV)

Our endurance not only produces good character here on earth, but has attached to it eternal benefit. "Here is a trustworthy saying: If we died with Him, we will also live with Him; if we endure, we will also reign with Him. If we disown Him, He will also disown us; if we are faithless, He will remain faithful, for He cannot disown Himself." 2 Timothy 2:11-13 (NIV)

We can find strength to endure, even when circumstances are dire, because we know that God is always treating us as sons and daughters, even if it doesn't' feel like it at the time. Faith is an important ingredient in perseverance. "Endure hardship as discipline; God is treating you as sons. For what son is not disciplined by his father?" Hebrews 12:7 (NIV)

"Watch your life and doctrine closely. Persevere in them, because if you do, you will save both yourself and your hearers." 1 Timothy 4:16 (NIV)

"You need to persevere so that when you have done the will of God, you will receive what He has promised." Hebrews 10:36 (NIV)

8

VULNERABILITY & HUMILITY DECLARATION

Today I choose to love. I will risk the possibility of hurt and brokenness. It is worth it. I say no to a safe, dark, unbreakable, impenetrable and unredeemable heart. I will no longer hide behind the masks of religion or a false self.

I will share my life with other believers. I will not hide behind religious words and phrases. I will not pretend to be better than I am. I will not hide my true self behind a mask any longer in order to be accepted. God has not made me perfect, but He has made me His. I am the object of His love.

I will no longer say, "Just leave me alone". I choose to nurture the eternal part of my life—my relationship with God and with others. God made me not only so He could love me, but so I could love Him back and love others as I love myself.

When I am tempted to become self-protective, I will choose risk. I will expend my life for the Kingdom of God—I will risk the possibility of hurt in order to achieve true community and intimacy. I will walk by faith and not fear.

I will not waste any time or energy defending myself when I am mocked or maligned. I know there will be times, because Jesus suffered unjust accusation that I will suffer too. But I will not retaliate. I choose to see such persecution as "par for the course"—it happened to the prophets; it can happen to me.

As I draw near to God—as I am caught up in His incredible, relentless love for me, the following will be true in my life: I will no longer live for myself, but I will live to please Christ. I will not only love God, but I will love His people because He wants me to. I will answer the call to be vulnerable.

Christ gave His life for me, so I will give my life for others. Christ's love for me has the power to defeat my insecurities and give me the resource I need to love others. I love because He first loved me—and nothing can separate me from His love.

As He died so I embrace my cross daily; as He rose from the dead I get real life—not an imposter's life. Today I clothe myself with compassion, kindness, humility, gentleness and patience toward my brothers and sisters in Christ. I choose to have a tender, forgiving heart. I choose the risk of loving others. I trust in God, so why should I be afraid? God has my back. Today, I choose to be vulnerable.

8

VULNERABILITY & HUMILITY AFFIRMATION

T o love is to be vulnerable. Love anything, and your heart will certainly be wrung and possibly be broken. If you want to make sure of keeping it intact, you must give your heart to no one, not even to an animal. Wrap it carefully round with hobbies and little luxuries; avoid all entanglements; lock it up safe in the casket or coffin of your selfishness. But in that casket– safe, dark, motionless, airless – it will change. It will not be broken; it will become unbreakable, impenetrable, irredeemable... The only place outside Heaven where you can be perfectly safe from all the dangers...of love is Hell." C. S. Lewis

True community happens when we remove our masks, engage in meaningful conversations, open our hearts with vulnerability, share our lives authentically, welcome accountability, and allow tenderness to flow freely. People really do become brothers and sisters. "How wonderful, how beautiful, when brothers and sisters get along! That's where God commands the blessing, ordains eternal life." Psalm 133:1, 3 (MSG)

To be vulnerable means that we are capable of being wounded—that we are not self- protective. We are called to expend our lives for Jesus, not to save them—He is the savior. To be vulnerable means to be a risk-taker. Don't expend all your energy saving yourself, trust God.

"God blesses you when people mock you and persecute you and lie about you and say all sorts of evil things against you because you are My followers. Be happy about it! Be very glad! For a great reward awaits you in Heaven. And remember, the ancient prophets were persecuted in the same way." Matthew 5:11-12 (NLT)

"Therefore, as God's chosen people, holy and dearly loved, clothe yourselves with compassion, kindness, humility, gentleness and patience. Bear with each other and forgive whatever grievances you may have against one another. Forgive as the Lord forgave you. And over all these

virtues put on love, which binds them all together in perfect unity."
Colossians 3:12-14 (NIV)

"Is there any encouragement from belonging to Christ? Any comfort from
His love? Any fellowship together in the Spirit? Are your hearts tender and
compassionate? Then make me truly happy by agreeing wholeheartedly
with each other, loving one another, and working together with one mind
and purpose. Don't be selfish; don't try to impress others. Be humble,
thinking of others as better than yourselves. Don't look out only for your
own interests, but take an interest in others, too." Philippians 2:1-4 (NLT)

"I trust in God, so why should I be afraid? What can mere mortals do to
me?" Psalms 56:11 (NLT)

9

DEPENDENCY ON GOD DECLARATION

I am giving up my dependency on myself and turning to God. No longer will I act first, and then ask God to bless; instead, I will ask before acting. This does not mean I am taking a passive stance toward my life—it simply means that God always gets the opportunity to speak before I act.

I will look to see what the Father is doing and cooperate with Him. Especially in ministry, I have constantly caved in to the temptation to use method and formulae instead of being dependent on God. But no more. Today I will take the risk of waiting on God—of even looking foolish because I don't look like I have all the answers or the power. I will not rely on what has worked in the past, I will not appeal to my own success. I will rely on God.

I realize that I can do nothing in my own strength or power. I will not strive to produce fruit in my life. I look to God to produce fruit in my life—I will strive earnestly to keep firmly connected to Him just like a branch is connected to the vine. As I stay joined with Him I know that my life will naturally yield a great harvest of good works and righteousness.

I will seek to be in the center of God's will for my life—not acting presumptuously by planning my life without His guidance. I believe that God has not only spoken through the Scriptures, but that He will speak to me daily. I will listen for the inner impression of God's voice telling me whether to turn to the left or to the right. I will begin my day asking what works He has prepared in advance for me. I know that I cannot hear perfectly, so I will always trust the Scripture as a guiding plumb line to keep me in the truth.

I will not light my path by my own reason and understanding. When it is dark around me, I will not give in to the temptation to invent my own light. I will trust in the Lord. I will wait for Him and not allow fear or impatience to drive me to action without His guidance.

I will gain strength by waiting on God and not wear myself out by straining in my own limited strength. I will learn to wait patiently— not demanding that Heaven move along my own timetable. I will not be like Saul who lost his courage while waiting; I will be courageous and wait on the Lord. My life is now defined by my dependence on God and my determination to follow Him.

9

DEPENDENCY ON GOD AFFIRMATION

A s disciples of Jesus, we are to imitate the life that He lived while on the earth. Part of that life was His dependency on the Father—just as Christ only did what He saw the Father doing, so we should do the same. That means choosing not to act until we ask the Father what He is doing. "So, Jesus explained, 'I tell you the truth, the Son can do nothing by Himself. He does only what He sees the Father doing. Whatever the Father does, the Son also does.'" John 5:19 (NLT)

"Then Jesus said to His disciples, 'If any of you wants to be My follower, you must turn from your selfish ways, take up your cross, and follow Me.'" Matthew 16:24 (NLT)

"Yes, I am the vine; you are the branches. Those who remain in Me, and I in them, will produce much fruit. For apart from Me you can do nothing." John 15:5 (NLT)

We are always tempted to live in autonomy—to be self-governing and self-directed. But that is not how we are called to live. "Now listen, you who say, 'Today or tomorrow we will go to this or that city, spend a year there, carry on business and make money.' Why, you do not even know what will happen tomorrow. What is your life? You are a mist that appears for a little while and then vanishes. Instead, you ought to say, 'If it is the Lord's will, we will live and do this or that.'" James 4:13-15 (NIV)

"Your own ears will hear Him. Right behind you a voice will say, 'This is the way you should go,' whether to the right or to the left." Isaiah 30:21 (NLT)

"Yet, the strength of those who wait with hope in the Lord will be renewed. They will soar on wings like eagles. They will run and won't become weary. They will walk and won't grow tired." Isaiah 40:31 (GW)

"Wait patiently for the Lord. Be brave and courageous. Yes, wait patiently for the Lord." Psalms 27:14 (NLT)

We are not, as the Poet William Ernest Henley wrote, "I am the master of my fate: I am the captain of my soul". We are citizens of Heaven and under the express authority of Jesus Christ.

"Who among you fears the Lord and obeys His servant? Let those who walk in darkness and have no light trust the name of the Lord and depend upon their God. But all of you light fires and arm yourselves with flaming torches. So walk in your own light and among the torches you have lit. This is what you will receive from Me: you will be tormented." Isaiah 50:10-11 (GW)

"When Saul was about thirty years old, he went to Gilgal to fight the Philistines. The prophet Samuel gave Saul specific instructions to wait for him seven days. After a few days, Saul caved in to pressure from his army and offered a burnt offering—something only Samuel was supposed to do. Samuel suddenly showed up and said to Saul: 'You acted foolishly, you have not kept the command the Lord your God gave you; if you had, He would have established your kingdom over Israel for all time. But now your kingdom will not endure; the Lord has sought out a man after His own heart and appointed him leader of His people, because you have not kept the Lord's command.'" 1 Samuel 13:13-14 (NIV)

10

SURRENDER DECLARATION

I n the past I have thought that as a Christian, the harder I worked, the more I would be blessed. I tended to plan and do the things I thought God would like, asking Him to bless it. But no more. Today, I surrender my will to You Lord; I will no longer treat You as predictable and programmable.

Today I am going to become a learner again. I have acted as if leadership had to do with having all the answers, so I have approached the "subject" of God as an expert. I am beginning again, but this time not as an expert but as a novice. Today I surrender my opinions, conjecture and conclusions about You, Lord, and come to You as a student; a disciple.

I surrender my plans to You, Father, I submit myself to You—lock, stock and barrel. Your words are life to me.

I know that I am unable to give in to the fear of man and still surrender fully to God. I choose this day to submit myself to You regardless of the opinions of those who themselves have not surrender their lives fully to You. I will learn obedience through the suffering of my life—just as Jesus did.

I will no longer raise my fist to the heavens and declare, "my will be done!" Instead, I give myself to do Your will, Lord. Today and every day I will follow You wherever You lead. In worship I lift my hands to You Lord in surrender—where You lead, I will follow.

Just as wine controls the person who drinks too much of it—so I will drink fully of the Holy Spirit in order to be completely under God's influence. I will no longer choose the sobriety of choosing my own way—the way of self-determination and ego-centric living. Instead, my life is wholly surrendered to God. I belong to God; I am His and He is mine. All that I have, and all that I am is His. I surrender everything to You, Father.

10

SURRENDER AFFIRMATION

urrender to God! Resist the devil, and he will run from you." James 4:7 (CEV)

"The sinful mind is hostile to God. It does not submit to God's law, nor can it do so." Romans 8:7 (NIV)

"Moreover, we have all had human fathers who disciplined us and we respected them for it. How much more should we submit to the Father of our spirits and live!" Hebrews 12:9 (NIV)

God loved you and me so much that He willingly took on human flesh in the person of Jesus Christ, and chose obedience and surrender for us. As our living example, Christ first surrendered His divinity in order to give us a flesh and blood God that we could relate to (John 3). He then surrendered His divine privilege and "took the humble position of a slave and was born as a human being. When He appeared in human form, He humbled Himself in obedience to God and died a criminal's death on a cross." Philippians 2:5-8 (NLT) For every human rebellion against God, Jesus took upon His perfect sinless body the weight of humanity's failure to yield to God. Christ paved the way for our surrender.

So, if Christ has surrendered so much on our behalf, how much more should we be willing to sacrifice for Him? "Though He was God's Son, He learned trusting-obedience by what He suffered, just as we do. Then, having arrived at the full stature of His maturity and having been announced by God as high priest in the order of Melchizedek, He became the source of eternal salvation to all who believingly obey Him." Hebrews 5:8-10 (MSG)

Jesus exemplified this surrender up until His last hours before being unjustly and cruelly crucified on a cross. In His surrender, He showed His humanity by willingly putting down His own will to surrender His will to the Father. Jesus did that, and that's what He is after in us. God wants us to become image bearers of His son. In His darkest moment, Jesus struggled to surrender, and we should expect nothing less for ourselves. Is it hard? Well, just look how hard it was for Jesus. "He went on a little farther and bowed with His face to the ground, praying, 'My Father! If it is possible, let this cup of suffering be taken away from me. Yet I want Your will to be done, not mine.'" Matthew 26:39 (NLT)

As C. S. Lewis said, "The Son of God suffered unto the death, not that men might not suffer, but that their sufferings might be like His."

May all our sufferings be our transformation into the likeness of Jesus Christ.

THE 140

DAILY READINGS

"A compass will always point you to true north and if you follow its path, you will surely never reach what you seek, for you cannot survive the swamps, rivers, and chasms you must cross on your way. If, however, you take your time, plan, and find routes around these obstacles, you will almost always reach your goal." Abraham Lincoln

DAY 1

1 John 5:19 says, "We know that we are children of God and that the world around us is under the control of the evil one."

Perhaps you've seen the movie "The Matrix." In that movie the main character 'Neo' finds out that the life he thought he was living was only a dream. A whole city of people had been enslaved by machines and was living a lie.

Neo is awakened out of his sleep and his attachment to the machines and finds out that the real world is much different than the world he thought he knew. Although the real world is less safe and much harder than his dream world—he decides to champion the cause of setting others free from the dream world.

Our Christian life is not much different. Paul writes in his second letter to Corinth that "Satan, who is the god of this world, has blinded the minds of those who don't believe. They are unable to see the glorious light of the Good News. They don't understand this message about the glory of Christ, who is the exact likeness of God." We have all been a part of that dream world. When we were dead because of our disobedience and our many sins, God gave us life when He raised Christ from the dead. We've been taken out of the matrix and given new life in Christ.

So, we've been awakened from our sleep. Time is running out; God has not only called us to wake up but to awaken others as well. Time is short, the world is under the control of the evil one and we have our marching orders. Clothe yourself with the presence of the Lord Jesus, and rescue everyone you can.

DAY 2

2 Corinthians 5:17 says, "Therefore, if anyone is in Christ, he is a new creation; old things have passed away; behold, all things have become new."

As believers, are we to just ignore the past and press forward even if we have been sexually or physically abused? In Philippians three, Paul talks about forgetting those things that are behind, but in context he is talking about his victories not his defeats.

Part of having all things become new is that the cross sheds a new light not only before us, but upon our past. There is a dangerous assumption in the Church that somehow emotional health and spiritual maturity can be separated. Sometimes our inability to move beyond sinful behavior patterns is a direct result of some unhealed part of our past. The result is broken relationships, addictions and recurring sins.

Those unhealed parts can be like a ticking time bomb—something the enemy will suddenly set off in our lives to destroy our effectiveness, our witness, and our confidence before God.

Our prayer should be: "Lord, help us to grow up before we grow too old." As one believer put it, "I was a Christian for twenty-two years; but instead of being a twenty-two-year-old Christian, I was a one- year-old Christian twenty-two times! I just kept doing the same things over and over and over again."

Christian formation is absolutely central. We are never called to ignore the past; we need to apply the cross to all of it, realizing that it may take some real time and effort—and help from others.

We are a new creation in Christ. Babies are also new, but they are not grownup. Our old way of living is gone—our new life has come, but we must grow up into the freedom that Christ gives us.

DAY 3

A part of building trust in relationships is respecting the needs of others. 1 Peter 2:17 says, "Show proper respect to everyone." It is when you get really close that you have to work at respect. Remember the adage, "familiarity breeds contempt?" God reinforces this idea in Ephesians 5:33 when He has Paul write "A wife must respect her husband." God knows that contempt is easy to get in a close relationship. Remember Mical, David's wife? This lack of respect breaks down trust because you don't believe the other person has your best interest at heart. They are not 'safe.'

Respect is not ignorance of wrong. It means not making the other person an enemy; they are innocent until proven guilty. It means not measuring them according to their cumulative faults; not measuring them according to the way everyone else treats you. It means seeing them as a unique creation of God; a person for whom Christ died for. And sometimes—a person God has put in your life to help you grow up.

But God didn't just address wives, He also told husbands to "love their wives as you love yourself—love your wives as Christ loves the church and gave Himself up for her." I've heard men joke with one another about 'having to ask their wife' before they do something. Sometimes men are derided because they want to include their wives in every decision they make. In the face of Paul's words here, that is just wrong. We are to sacrifice, literally lay down our lives for our wives.

In I Peter 3, we are told "treat your wife with respect so that nothing will hinder your prayers." God knows that our relationships here on earth are crucial—you cannot be one kind of person with people and another kind with God. If you are shallow with people, whom you can see, you will be shallow with God who is unseen. That is one reason why our relationships with people are so important to God. He knows that if we aren't real with people, we won't be real with Him.

DAY 4

A patient in a Jerusalem' French Hospital in 1956, who was also a nun, was looking out of a window in West Jerusalem looking towards East Jerusalem (which was then occupied by Jordanian soldiers). She was at the very edge of West Jerusalem looking down on the barbed wire and rubble of the non-man's land between Israel and Jordan. She was looking at the walls of the Old City, and the Jordanian soldiers looked down from the ramparts.

Suddenly she sneezed, or coughed so hard that her false teeth shot out of her mouth and fell into the rubble in no-man's land. She was distressed and wanted her teeth back. She approached the Israeli military and asked them to retrieve her teeth. They said it was impossible as anybody entering the no-man's land would be shot. But as she persisted, the Israeli military said they would see what they could do.

The Israeli military asked the United Nations if it could help. The UN approached the Jordanian military, and eventually it was agreed that a combined force of Israeli and Jordanian soldiers under the leadership of the UN would try and retrieve the teeth. A few soldiers emerged from each side, and under the white flag held by the UN peacekeeper they searched the rubble together—and they found the nun's teeth.

Peace, such a tenuous and fragile thing, is sometimes accomplished through simple events unrelated to the fuss everyone is embroiled in. My prayer is that we may be distracted long enough from the boiling circumstances of life, even by something outrageous like a search for false teeth, to find peace in the presence of One who's joy is being known as "The Prince of Peace." In His simple and humble way, may He always be the great distraction from the mundane hand-wringing we so often find ourselves entangled in.

"For to us a child is born, to us a son is given, and the government will be on his shoulders. And he will be called Wonderful Counselor, Mighty God, Everlasting Father, Prince of Peace."
Isaiah 9:6 (NIV)

DAY 5

A person's wisdom yields patience; it is to one's glory to overlook an offense." Proverbs 19:11 (NIV)

T he good news is that the gospel doesn't make us less human, but more human. As followers of Jesus, we experience the full range of disappointments and emotions common to all image bearers of God. But, by God's grace, we can learn to steward them rather than live as slaves to them. We can learn to respond as redemptively as possible, as opposed to reacting selfishly and self-righteously. And we can actually find joy when we "overlook an offense."

But first, let's be clear: overlooking an offense must not be confused with submitting to abusive people or morally and ethically unacceptable circumstances. Jesus calls us to be foot washers, not doormats.

The apostle Paul comments on this in Romans 16:17-18:

"Now I urge you, brethren, note those who cause divisions and offenses, contrary to the doctrine which you learned, and avoid them. For those who are such do not serve our Lord Jesus Christ, but their own belly, and by smooth words and flattering speech deceive the hearts of the simple."

In this passage, Paul instructs church leaders to note those who create offenses. In the King James Version, the phrase "note those" is translated as "mark those." Paul is emphasizing that church leaders should publicly identify those who cause division or offense.

The act of "marking" someone signifies a serious form of disfellowshipping from the church. While disfellowshipping is typically handled in private, marking indicates that the individual's actions are so severe that they need to be brought to the attention of the entire congregation. This highlights the gravity of the sin of causing offense if it remains unresolved.

DAY 6

According to oral history, dishonest sculptors in Greece and Rome would cover flaws in their work by using wax. If the sculpture was chipped, cracked or damaged the dishonest sculptors would melt wax into the marble dust, using it to conceal the flaw or imperfection.

In ancient Rome, sculpting was a popular profession. The market was flooded with sculptors, so quality was sometimes lacking. Less qualified craftsmen would cover their flaws and errors in wax, and frequently the customer could not see the cover-up. To compensate for this practice, authentic sculptors would mark their statutes with the words "sine cere," which means, "without wax." Today, we frequently use the same term to close our letters: "sincerely."

It is so easy in our "fast-food" world to be tempted to take shortcuts. It is hard to wait. The Apostle Paul wrote to the Christians at Ephesus, "Don't be foolish, but understand what the Lord's will is. Don't get drunk on wine which leads to wild living, instead, be filled (the word literally means to "keep on being filled") with the Spirit." Ephesians 5:17-18 (GW)

Our work will not earn us one moment of eternity—that was bought with the blood of Jesus. However, once you become a Christian you are called to the long obedience of following Jesus. But it is not work as we often think of it. It is nurturing the life of Christ inside us. That is not as easy as it sounds. It is so much easier to fill our lives with the appearance of being like Him, rather than going deep to truly become like Him. In fact, to really be like Him, we must die to ourselves.

What we die to is our inauthentic parts—like the errors on Roman sculptures that were fixed with wax. God wants to mark us "sine cere"; sincere followers of Christ that don't cover up their flaws with the wax of religious language or actions. God wants a real and genuine people who follow a real and authentic God.

May we, His people, be people of integrity.

"Lord, who may dwell in your sacred tent? Who may live on your holy mountain? The one whose walk is blameless, who does what is righteous, who speaks the truth from their heart." Psalm 15:1-2 (NIV)

DAY 7

"And now we live in fellowship with the true God because we live in fellowship with His Son, Jesus Christ. He is the only true God, and He is eternal life." 1 John 5:20 (NLT)

T o hear some people talk, Christianity is just fire insurance—give your life to Jesus and get Heaven instead of hell in the end.

When you get married, you repent of the way you have been living (as a single person), and promise to turn from that and be faithful to your spouse. That is repentance; to turn from one direction and go another. But once you have made that vow and married your spouse, it is not okay to live single—saying that all that mattered was that you repented in the beginning. Marriage may begin as an event, but it goes on as a million choices.

Of course, there are times when we stray from our vows and act like single people, but repentance is what brings us back to the relationship. The relationship is what is important. We cannot keep going back to the marriage ceremony as evidence of our marriage. Marriage is based on an ongoing commitment—and that commitment can only be sustained by continued repentance.

The same is true with God. Confession and repentance are the ways we get in and the way we go on. Salvation is not some event where we made a deal with God then we will see Him later. If we cannot rely upon God in this life, how could we rely upon Him in the next? So many are guilty of looking like believers, but lack the real fruit of discipleship.

The gospel is not the "great arrangement", like a get out of jail free card. It is the good news of the presence and availability of life in the Kingdom, now and forever. If we know Jesus now, we will be with Him forever. That is eternal life.

DAY 8

"and she gave birth to her firstborn, a son. She wrapped Him in cloths and placed Him in a manger, because there was no room for them in the inn." Luke 2:7 (NIV)

F ear and worship traditionally go hand in hand. Sacrifices are offered to appease the gods. Kneeling Muslims must bow so low that their foreheads touch the ground. Jews could not even pronounce or spell the name of God. They offered sacrifices to appease Him. There was the sacred mountain that those who touched it would die. There was the voice of God so powerful that the people begged Moses to serve as mediator so they wouldn't have to hear it. Mishandle the ark of God and you die. Enter the Holy Place and lose your life.

In all this, God came lowly in a stable. He arrived with no royal fanfare, no parades, and in no fancy palace. In Jesus, God related to mankind in a way that did not involve fear. He came not to emphasize the gulf between God and mankind, but to span it. The Word became flesh like us, God became someone we could relate to in a more familiar way. One of the greatest, most mysterious and powerful miracles of all time, God becoming one of us, arrived.

This is not the kind of God we could have invented. He is sometimes puzzling, often mysterious, harsh, kind, loving, warm, and distant to us. Some of that is our mis-understanding. But in Jesus, God wants to reveal Himself to us in a new way. It is the new covenant—which doesn't replace the old but fulfills it. God in Jesus is telling us and showing us new things about Himself that we didn't know or understand before. Can we see it? Does it stretch us? This revelation of God in Jesus Christ is the way God wants to relate to us. How privileged we are!

The Old Testament with its displays of God's glory and His wrath all pointed towards this revelation—God never had to lower His love to exercise His wrath or vice versa. He is always fully Himself—never more, never less. As Christians we fear God, but we are never afraid of Him; in His presence we feel overwhelmed and undone and yet there is no place we would rather be.

If your idea of God is that He is some kind of cosmic tyrant, then you need to read the Bible through the lens of this supernatural birth. God invaded our rebellious world as a new born baby rather than as an army destroying everything in its path. The most powerful being in the universe makes Himself vulnerable on our behalf and for our benefit. As C. S. Lewis once said, "The Son of God became a man that men might become sons of God." Now that's some good news!

DAY 9

"Anyone who hates his brother is a murderer, and you know that no murderer has eternal life in him." 1 John 3:15 (NIV)

An unkind remark or a lapse in sensitivity might seem like a minor issue considering our capabilities, or even acceptable, if one were to view the world from our perspective. The problem is, we can often be contemptful without considering the damage we are doing to another person. Our perspective is colored by a myriad of experiences and can be affected by how we feel, what we ate last night, or some difficulty we are going through.

Contempt is a way of degrading a person without being honestly up- front. It is justified in our minds as "they deserve my contempt" because of how they have acted or failed to act. It excuses the sin of rage and degrading or demeaning others by being sneaky. But it is still a kind of soul murder.

The part of shame that lies beneath our contempt has more to do with not being humiliated than having an actual offense. The idea that we may not be smart enough, or adequate enough (whatever the task), to even be in the same room as some people can drive our contempt. We keep our heads low knowing we are not the smartest person in the room, but we like to keep it above the heads of lesser mortals, usually by demeaning those who might be as or more competent than we are. Many people find contempt as a useful tool to exalt themselves on the backs of others, while not committing an overt offense.

When we are finding fault with others and not exercising love, we often act in contempt. Contempt is insidious because it can hide behind the veneer of a smile. It can even masquerade as a joke, but is never funny to the one who is the object of contempt.

In fact, contempt is very much like a bloodless stiletto that stabs one in the back and slowly drains the life out of their soul. It is a "private murder" because it is difficult to discern.

DAY 10

A s a believer, God has purposes for your life. Each of us has a mission. Our common mission is to tell people the good news about God's grace.

God wants me TO SHARE THE GOOD NEWS. Once I know that God is in control, that God made me in order to love me, that life is not an accident and it has a purpose—then God expects me to share that with others.

"Evangelism" is very misunderstood. We sometimes think of guys with big hair shouting "SEND ME YOUR MONEY!" That's not good news to anybody except the guys with big hair. But evangelism is really 'good news'. And here is it: God loves me and has a plan for my life. The way I grew up, you would think evangelism is all bad news: They said: "GOD WANTS TO SEND YOU TO HELL IF YOU DON'T SHAPE UP." The truth is that the Bible says in 2 Peter 3:9 that God doesn't want anyone to perish, but everyone to come to repentance.

"the lord is not slow in keeping his promise, as some understand slowness. He is patient with you, not wanting anyone to perish, but everyone to come to repentance." 1 Peter 3:9

So where do we share? If we use the model of Acts 1:8, we begin at home, then next door, then to the ends of the earth.

God doesn't call us to be His defense attorney, His prosecutor, or His salesman. He just wants you to tell what you've seen, and what has happened to you. You are the best authority on your life.

God wants us to partner with Him to plunder hell and populate Heaven. We don't have to be experts to do that. We do best when we simply and honestly share with others what God has done to us and for us, and what He means to us. Evangelism is one beggar telling another beggar where to find fresh bread.

DAY 11

As a child, I used to imagine that my toys could come to life—long before there were any movies to give me that idea. I would sometimes talk to them as if they could hear me. I would imagine that we would do some daring exploits together. I would like you to imagine with me what it would be like to have one of your little toys turn into a real person.

You might tell them all the things they could do with their bodies of flesh that they could not do with bodies of moldable material. You could tell them of touch and taste and smell. But what happens when their bodies begin to turn into flesh? I don't think they'd like it. They wouldn't understand—all they would see is that their current state is being ruined. Maybe they think they are dying.

Now that is what Christ has done. He became one of us to make us real. That hard work of becoming real or alive could not be done by us, so Christ came and did it for us. We don't have to try to climb up into some spiritual life by our own efforts—the spiritual life has already come down to us in Christ. All we have to do is lay ourselves open to the One Real Person in whom true spiritual life was fully present, and He will do it for us.

But sometimes in this process we may feel like He is killing us. All we can see is that our ugly false self is being ruined; our self-centeredness, our pride, our lust and rebellion. And all this talk about trying to be good enough for God is just as silly as a toy trying to act like it's real. Christianity is not about reforming the old and making it better; it is about transforming the old into something totally new and different. You will never be the same.

These thoughts are inspired by C. S. Lewis

"God wanted to make known among the Gentiles the glorious wealth of this mystery, which is Christ in you, the hope of glory."
Colossians 1:27 (CSB)

57

DAY 12

"I make known the end from the beginning, from ancient times, what is still to come. I say, 'My purpose will stand, and I will do all that I please.'" Isiah 46:10

A s C. S. Lewis says through a character in his book, "Aslan (the symbolic creature of Christ in the story) is not a tame lion. God doesn't fit in our boxes. Eventually He will save those He saves and damn those He damns and if we are not okay with that then we have very little understanding of true nature of God. But from our end, we just don't know. So, we have to go about the business of the Kingdom as if everyone we meet is potentially a fit for Heaven, and we must help them all we can, while we can, lest they die on our watch and are lost because we damned them before their time."

Is the church today known for its salvific work, or its condemnation and criticism? The reality is one part of the church is known for "easy grace", that is, that somehow all will be saved in the end regardless of their belief or actions, while simultaneously another part of the church believes they are the only ones saved because of their perfect theology.

The Bible clearly teaches we are saved by grace—believing and trusting in God's salvation through Jesus Christ His son. We are responsible for our actions. We are responsible for our choices. If we can live this life any way that we want without regards to the consequence of hell—then we are truly not free at all. The choice was made for us.

And as Christians, our failure to cooperate with the Spirit of God will keep us from growing in sanctification, or holiness, or character (which is another way to say Christ—likeness).

Christianity is not magic, and it is not what you would expect. *God chooses to do what He does* (I will do all that I please), and it is okay because He is always love, He always executes proper judgment, and He is always holy. He allows us to choose to be with Him or not. That's the gospel truth!

DAY 13

"Forget the former things; do not dwell on the past. See, I am doing a new thing! Now it springs up; do you not perceive it? I am making a way in the desert and streams in the wasteland." Isaiah 43:18-19 (NIV)

T the idea of not looking back is a recurring theme in the Bible, and it's often used to encourage people to keep moving forward in faith and trust in God. A good example comes from the story of Lot's wife in Genesis 19. God, before destroying Sodom, instructed Lot's family to flee without looking back. Lot's wife, clinging to her past life, looked back and transformed into a pillar of salt. This tragedy warns that Lot's wife, fixated on a doomed past, had the wrong priorities.

In the New Testament, Jesus says in Luke 9:62, "No one who puts a hand to the plow and looks back is fit for service in the Kingdom of God." He is suggesting that if we're focused on the past, we're not engaged in the present or the future that God has in store for us. Focusing solely on the task ahead ensures straight rows; frequent glances backward create disorder.

To heal, we must at times confront past hurts, inviting Jesus in to bring us into giving and receiving forgiveness. You cannot withhold forgiving yourself, as some do, saying they do not deserve forgiveness. If God forgives you, who are you to walk in unforgiveness with yourself?

The past, with all its mistakes and victories, doesn't have to dictate our future. By focusing on God's promises and staying present in His will, we can move forward with hope, knowing that He's guiding us toward something better.

DAY 14

"At the sixth hour darkness came over the whole land until the ninth hour." Mark 15:33 (NIV)

T hese are the last three hours of Jesus on the cross. From noon until three, darkness covered the land.

Jesus had been arrested and tried. Peter had denied ever knowing Him. The disciples were helpless before the power of the Pharisees and Sadducees, and especially before the iron hand of Rome. Their Rabbi, their Lord and King had been crucified. The darkness of these hours was more than the absence of sunlight. There was a darkness that had crept into the hearts of the disciples. After three hours of afternoon darkness the Messiah had died on a cross.

Jesus had told them this time was coming. He warned them but in the dark, they lost their way. He had tried to tell them He was going away and would send the Spirit to be with them. He told them plainly that He would be handed over to be crucified. But when the darkness came, they forgot what He had said to them.

After Jesus was buried, the disciples went back to their old lives. Some went fishing. They had experienced an incredible shock. But that was nothing to what they were about to experience. Not only had Christ warned them of His death; but He had also said after three days He would rise again.

Then He did.

It is perhaps too easy for us to see the failings of the disciples from this viewpoint. But we can learn from their mistakes. The darkness may seem impenetrable at times, but it won't last. God will often instruct us before the darkness comes. And we should never doubt in the dark what God has spoken to us in the light.

DAY 15

"Dear friends, do not believe every spirit, but test the spirits to see whether they are from God, because many false prophets have gone out into the world." 1 John 4!1 (NIV 84)

W ere there seasons when God spoke directly to the entire nation of Israel so that they personally heard His voice? Doesn't it seem like He almost always uses a human mediator in which He speaks to His people? What are the specific exceptions to this? Children of Israel at the Mount of Sinai who heard a voice; in the N. T. people around Jesus hear a voice from Heaven but it was not necessarily directed to just believers. Peter speaks for God at Pentecost, James, John, Paul, Matthew, and Luke, all spoke to the church in the New Testament.

All this has become somewhat of a mess in some of the Charismatic circles of Christianity. People who object to the idea that God is always chatting to individuals in the church are razed as faithless and feckless Christians (even their Christianity is questioned!).

Leaders who question those in the Church who claim superiority because of how well they hear God are demonized and accused of wanting control, of wanting to shut down the Spirit of God, and of being ego-centric. "We all have the same Spirit in us!" is the rallying cry, along with, "the same Spirit that lived in Paul lives in me, so I can do anything he did." They want everyone on the same footing as themselves, or sometimes maybe a little lower than themselves. But while we all get in the same way; we don't all carry on the same.

There is a great need for the rise of discernment in the church today. Discernment is the dissidence of an unfamiliar or unwelcomed sound.

In fact, I would rather see mature discernment than even the greatest gifts of prophecy or miracles. Why? Because discernment is the only thing that can distinguish between the authentic and the false. True godliness is not manifested as power; it is manifested in humble service and laser—like discernment. The need for character development in the church is at an all- time high.

My prayer for you is for that powerful discernment that is framed by love, as Paul writes in his letter to the Philippians:

"And this is my prayer: that your love may abound more and more in knowledge and depth of insight, so that you may be able to discern what is best and may be pure and blameless until the day of Christ." Philippians 1:9-10 (NIV 84)

DAY 16

"How priceless is your unfailing love, O God! People take refuge in the shadow of your wings." Psalm 36:7 (NIV)

Billy was raised in an angry family. Mealtimes were either silent or sarcastically noisy. They often ended in arguments and tears. He usually got yelled at if he spilled any food or drink on the table, or if he didn't finish his food, or if he slumped at the table—it seemed as though he couldn't do anything right.

When Billy was about ten, he began excusing himself from the dinner table (as soon as he could without being yelled at) and walking down the street to a neighbor's house.

The old-fashioned house down the street had a big porch on the outside and a happy family inside. If Billy arrived there during dinnertime, he would crawl under the porch and sit there quietly, listening to the sounds of warmth and laughter.

One day Billy was invited in for dinner. He was so excited and so nervous that when he reached to receive some rolls from the person next to him, he accidentally spilled his milk. He would have shrunk into his napkin if he could. He waited for the expected verbal blow. Instead, the father stood up, and with a roar of delight cried, "get the boy some more milk and a dry shirt. I want him to enjoy this meal!"

Billy's experience showed him that not all fathers are angry and harsh. We often get our ideas of what God the Father is like through our experiences with our earthly fathers. But even the best earthly father cannot love us with a perfect love like our heavenly Father can. We need to look at the Scriptures to get an accurate picture of what God the Father is like. Let Him surprise you with His love in the pages of the Bible; just let Him speak to your heart.

My prayer for you is the prayer the Apostle Paul prayed for the people of the Church of Ephesus:

"I pray that out of his glorious riches he may strengthen you with power through his Spirit in your inner being, so that Christ may dwell in your hearts through faith. And I pray that you, being rooted and established in love, may have power, together with all the Lord's holy people, to grasp how wide and long and high and deep is the love of Christ, and to know this love that surpasses knowledge—that you may be filled to the measure of all the fullness of God." Ephesians 3:18-19 (NIV)

DAY 17

"Blessed are the meek." Matthew 5:5 (NIV)

W hen God blesses the meek, He is not blessing mousy, wimpy, whining people. The word "meek" means, "not fighting against God." It means to lay down your arms and surrender, to stop rebelling. In the Garden of Eden, Adam and Eve basically shook their fists in the face of God and said, "not your will but our will be done".

We must surrender ourselves to God, saying "You are God and we are not." It's time we stop dictating to God what we like and don't like; what we will and will not do; what we want and what we don't want. Worship itself is surrender to God. Raising our hands to God in worship is a physical expression of our surrender. In worship we say: "we give ourselves to You, God; our minds, our bodies, and our hearts. All of us to all of You." You cannot partially surrender. It is all or nothing. God asks for unconditional surrender.

To walk humbly with God is to not fight against Him. Blessed are the meek—those who don't contend with God. Whenever we resist God, we bow down before the devil; there is no middle ground. James chapter four says that if you draw close to God, God will draw near to you. James then calls us to clean up our hearts and to not be double-minded. In other words, don't try to ride the fence.

There is a story from World War II about a man in a European town who carried two flags in his back pocket: one German, and the other American. His intention was to wait until he found out who occupied the town, and then fly the winning flag. When Jesus returns, it will be too late to decide, and besides, God will know that that kind of surrender is a lie. Now is the time, don't wait and even think you can fool God about surrender. Don't put off your surrender to God for even one more hour.

DAY 18

"But just as you excel in everything--in faith, in speech, in knowledge, in complete earnestness and in your love for us--see that you also excel in this grace of giving." 2 Corinthians 8:7 (NIV)

I t is just as important to excel in giving as it is to excel in our praise and worship. We should be known as the most generous people in the world. We are not just the people who worship well, or heal the sick—our generosity should reflect the generosity of God.

And we should view giving as a great privilege. "They urgently pleaded with us for the privilege of sharing in this service to the saints." 2 Corinthians 8:4 (NIV) When was the last time you thanked God for the opportunity of giving?

God dramatically releases His love and grace into the lives of cheerful and generous givers. This is not magic or an investment in the stock market. God's design is: sow sparingly, reap sparingly. In His heart, God loves a cheerful (hilarious) giver. As you give generously, you are defying everything that Satan stands for—you are refusing to be held captive by his doctrines. Let God be true—He will supply all our needs according to His riches in glory—and let every man be a liar.

Let's look at this passage: "This is the day the Lord has made; We will rejoice and be glad in it. Save now, I pray, O Lord; O Lord, I pray, send now prosperity." Psalm 118:24-25 (NKJV)

The Hebrew word for prosperity literally means: "To push forward and break out." Don't let yourself be kept from God's purposes for your life. Don't let the hand of the enemy overrule the hand of God. Ask God to empower you to push forward and break out of the bondage the enemy has kept you in. Ask God to make you generous!

DAY 19

C. S. Lewis once said, "Once in our world, a stable had something in it that was bigger than our whole world." — The Last Battle

L ewis also related a story from his brother Warren, "My brother heard a woman on a bus say, as the bus passed a church with a crib outside it … 'They bring religion into everything. Look, they're dragging it even into Christmas now.'" — Personal correspondence

The first living nativity scene is generally ascribed to St. Francis of Assisi. On December 24, 1223, he found a cave near Greccio, Italy, and brought in animals traditionally associated with the birth of Christ. Francis was known for his love of animals, and had even been known to preach to them. He built a manger, arranged the hay, and arranged the animals. Crowds gathered in curiosity, and then awe while there on Christmas Eve Francis preached the wonder of God made man; born a helpless infant and laid in the manger. "Behold your God," he said, "a poor and helpless child, the ox and donkey beside Him. Your God is of your flesh."

Francis had been born in 1182 in central Italy and was the son of a wealthy merchant. After a meager education, he joined the army and became a prisoner of war. He put his faith in Christ shortly after his release, and soon began traveling around the countryside preaching the gospel. His father, indignant at his son's choices, tried in vain to change Francis' mind. Francis eventually renounced his father and his inheritance.

At a Mass in February of 1209, Francis became gripped by the words being read from Matthew's gospel: "The Kingdom of Heaven is near. Heal the sick, raise the dead, cleanse those who have leprosy, drive out demons. Freely you have received, freely give. Do not take along any gold or silver or copper in your belts; take no bag for the journey, or extra tunic or sandals or a staff."

Francis felt Christ speaking directly to him. He took those words to heart and decided to obey them as literally as possible, choosing a life of poverty and dedicating himself to the poor, making himself a living testament to Jesus. The Kingdom of Heaven is near.

DAY 20

"Come near to God, and he will come near to you. Clean up your lives, you sinners. Purify your hearts, you people who can't make up your mind." James 4:8 (CEV)

C. S. Lewis talks about nearness to God in two ways: nearness of approach and likeness to God.

In likeness to God, humans were created in the image of God. Through the fall, that image has been marred—much like an image is distorted in a defective mirror. We imperfectly reflect a perfect God.

Nearness in approach has to do with the state of humans as they seek God and find Him through the salvation that is freely offered in Christ.

He uses an analogy. Let's suppose that we are doing a mountain walk to our home village. At noon we come to the top of a cliff where we are very near it because it is just below us. We could drop a stone into it. But there is no way to get directly down to the village because we have no equipment and we are no mountain climbers. We must take a long way around, ten miles maybe. At many points during that detour, we will, spatially, be farther from the village than we were when we sat above the cliff. But only spatially. In terms of progress, we will be far nearer our home.

God does not want us sitting on the cliff counting on our likeness to Him to get us to Him. We may think we are good enough, but there is no way to get to Him from there. We don't have the equipment— and we don't have the skill. The only way to God is the path around—the path through the cross. That's why God wants us to seek Him; He doesn't want us to rest on our feelings of being near enough. He wants us to go down the only real path in which He can be found.

DAY 21

"He who did not spare his own Son, but gave him up for us all—
how will he not also, along with him, graciously give us all
things?" Romans 8:32 (NIV)

C harles Spurgeon, the great English preacher, told this story from his pulpit in London:

A woman had been hired by a very rich man to take care of his household. She served the rich man faithfully for over twenty years. When the wealthy man was about to die, he called the poor woman to his bedside and thanked her for her faithfulness to him. He had no heirs, and therefore decided to be generous to the woman. He wrote something on a piece of paper and handed it to her. She was grateful for this act of remembrance on his part.

She lived in a little shack on the outskirts of the city of London. She took the piece of paper home and pinned it up on the wall. Several years later she became sick and Spurgeon was called to visit her.

After he prayed for her, he walked around the room and noticed this piece of paper on the wall. He turned to the woman and asked her about it and she told him the story. He added, "Can you read?"

She said, "No, I have never been taught how to read."

And then he said, "Madam, this piece of paper is a check for a great deal of money. You did not have to be living in these poor circumstances. You could have been living in the finest houses in London, eating the finest foods."

The Scriptures tell us that when we first put our faith in Jesus Christ, He placed His Holy Spirit in our lives to give us all the resources of Heaven. The Holy Spirit in the life of the believer is like a blank check that God has written and signed, all we need to do is cash it.

DAY 22

"Fallen man is not simply an imperfect creature who needs improvement: he is a rebel who must lay down his arms. Laying down your arms, surrendering, saying you are sorry, realising that you have been on the wrong track and getting ready to start life over again from the ground floor—that is the only way out of our 'hole'. This process of surrender—this movement full speed astern—is what Christians call repentance." C. S. Lewis

David Platt writes, "The modern-day gospel says, 'God loves you and has a wonderful plan for your life. Therefore, follow these steps, and you can be saved.' Meanwhile, the biblical gospel says, 'You are an enemy of God, dead in your sin, and in your present state of rebellion, you are not even able to see that you need life, much less to cause yourself to come to life. Therefore, you are radically dependent on God to do something in your life that you could never do.

The truth is what we want is a 'nice, middle class American Jesus.' A Jesus who doesn't mind materialism and who would never call us to give away everything we have. A Jesus who would not expect us to forsake our closest relationships so that He receives all our affection. A Jesus who is okay with nominal devotion that does not infringe on our comforts, because, after all, as the saying goes, 'He loves us just the way we are.' A Jesus who wants us to be balanced, who wants us to avoid dangerous extremes, and who, for that matter, wants us to avoid danger altogether. A Jesus who brings us comfort and prosperity as we live out our Christian spin on the American dream."

But here we are molding Jesus into our own image. He is beginning to look just like us. What's so frightening is that we may not be worshipping the Jesus of the Bible at all; we may just be worshipping a caricature of ourselves.

It is true that Jesus loves us just the way we are, but He is determined not to leave us in the state we are in.

DAY 23

"We also know that the Son of God has come and has given us understanding so that we may know the true God. We are in union with the one who is true, his Son Jesus the Messiah, who is the true God and eternal life." 1 John 5:20 (NSV)

D eath for the believer is to be present with the Lord. We know that Jesus is eternal life according to 1 John 5:20.

Christ is the boss over death. In Revelation 1:18 (NLT) He says, "I am the living one who died. Look, I am alive forever and ever! And I hold the keys of death and the grave." As Ron Dunn has said, "The devil doesn't have the keys to his own house! The keys are a symbol of authority, of control, of possession and government. As terrible as it is, death is not allowed to run rampant without control. Nothing happens by chance. All history lies in the elective purpose of God. Even death is in the hands of God. It moves only at the permissive will of Heaven."

Christ holds the key to death, and no man enters it unless our Lord Jesus uses the key and opens it.

Death is not just good-bye for Christians. It is also saying hello to the Lord Jesus and to our Christian friends and relatives who have died before us.

In *The Applause of Heaven*, Max Lucado ends his book with these words to all who have accepted Jesus Christ as Savior and Lord: "Before you know it, your appointed arrival time will come; you'll descend the ramp and enter the City. You'll see faces that are waiting for you. You'll hear your name spoken by those who love you. And maybe, just maybe-in the back, behind the crowds-the One who would rather die than live without you will remove His pierced hands from His heavenly robe and... *applaud.*"

We have been dying since the day we were born. The last thing death is for us is unnatural. It was said of the early followers of John Wesley, "they die well." May that be said of all of us as well.

DAY 24

Deuteronomy 8:3 (NIV) says, "He humbled you, causing you to hunger and then feeding you with manna, which neither you nor your fathers had known, to teach you that man does not live on bread alone but on every word that comes from the mouth of the Lord."

S ometimes we Christians look more like goats than sheep, at least as far as our eating habits are concerned—especially regarding spiritual food. It seems like we are willing to feed on anything except every word that comes from the mouth of the Lord.

As Americans we are often addicted to spiritual junk food. We gladly feed on news, movies, TV, sports and entertainment—drugs and alcohol are certainly not the only escapes we use. In fact, nearly any distraction will do—feeding on our relationship with Jesus is often the last thing we think of.

In *The Lion, The Witch, and The Wardrobe*, a book from C. S. Lewis' series *The Chronicles of Narnia*, the young boy Edmond is fed a "magic junk food" called "Turkish Delight" by the White Witch. It tastes wonderful, and even makes his fingers sticky, but it never, ever satisfies his hunger.

That is the nature of spiritual junk food—it seems to feed a need in the moment, but it never satisfies—it always leaves your stomach empty and wanting more. And even worse, it gives you no strength for the journey and no energy for the fight.

God allowed the Israelites to hunger so that He could feed them bread from Heaven. God is still in the business of making His people hungry. May we, in our hunger, find our nourishment in Jesus, the Bread of Life! We all have a God-shaped hole inside us that only Jesus can fill.

DAY 25

Discernment is more important than gifting (discerning of spirits is a different thing that I won' go into here). People often talk about hearing God say this, and God said that. I've had people tell me how God constantly talks to them and tells them everything every day. It is true that if you brush your teeth every day, you will probably end up with a nice full set in your old age. But nothing in Scripture leads me to believe that while that is true, and that God *really* loves me, He's not in the business of telling me to brush my teeth every morning. That's just not "God-like".

And someone may argue that it is irresponsible for me to say what I believe is "God-like" or not, but the reality is that we should be so immersed in Scripture that not only are we able to discern when God is speaking or not, and that we come to know Him well where we are able to say, "that doesn't like something God would say". Of course, we have to be careful that we develop and good sense of who God is because we can't afford to brush things off because they make us feel uncomfortable; such as the prophet Isaiah having to cook his food over dung, or God telling Abraham to sacrifice his son. But that is the point, God speaks with purpose when He speaks to us and it is more about His purposes than ours.

I heard a nationally known prophet once say that God is constantly speaking and we just have to "tune" into that frequency, kind of like tuning a radio in to a particular channel that God is speaking on.

But God is not "chatty." All throughout the Bible God speaks to individuals on certain occasions, but for His purposes—not for our moment by moment need to be directed by God. It is tempting to add the tag "God told me" to everything we do so that we don't have to carry any personal responsibility for our actions.

Occasionally God gave specific directions to individuals, but it was not a play-by-play plan for what He had for them. In fact, in the case of Abraham, God told him to go—to leave his home. He didn't even tell him where to go!

Then you have Phillip in the New Testament being told by the Spirit of God to go to this certain place, and see this certain man, etc., etc. But you also have Paul who just goes on his mission and is driving so hard that once the Spirit had to prevent him, once Satan prevented him, and he had a vision of a Macedonian calling to him to come. He knew he was going to Rome and was gonna face real trouble, but he didn't know when and he didn't seem interested in storming Heaven to find out.

Does God speak to His people? Absolutely, yes. But in the Bible, it never seems like a running dialogue. People have taken a few verses (you will hear a voice saying, walk this way...My sheep hear My voice and know Me...God will give you words to speak), but they are always in context of something particular. We are friends of God, but He is never our buddy. If we want to represent God well, let us know Him well enough to get it right.

DAY 26

"Do not lie to each other, since you have taken off your old self with its practices and have put on the new self, which is being renewed in knowledge in the image of its Creator." Colossians 3:9-10 (NIV)

T he first part of building trust is being honest with each other. Lies are told in the absence of trust—if we think the truth will not be beneficial then we may begin to lie.

In the Garden of Eden, Eve was tempted to not trust God by the serpent. He appealed to something in all of us that is prone to distrust. In effect, he said "God does not have your best interest at heart; He has a hidden agenda that is to keep you in your place." So, trust is hard for us to build. We are a suspicious lot.

But why are we so quick to lie? Truth told; we have much to hide. We will often exert more energy hiding the truth than it would take to tell the truth. Why? We don't want people to know what we are really like because they may reject us or pressure us to change. We like hiding behind lies; usually not big ones, just the little ones we like to call "white lies." But it is still a falsehood, even if a little one. We can't ever trust each other if we tell each other lies.

So how do we cross this bridge? Begin small. Start with one safe person and have an honest talk. Show them the real you—not some pretend person. As your relationships become more authentic—they will become healthier. They will challenge you and change you. They will become a part of God's plan to mold you into the image of Jesus. Telling lies can become the avalanche that literally smothers your life. There is real freedom and peace in truth telling.

DAY 27

"Do nothing out of selfish ambition or vain conceit, but in humility consider others better than yourselves. Each of you should look not only to your own interests, but also to the interests of others." Philippians 2:3-4 (NIV)

None of us should want to build our own ministries; it is up to God to do that. God calls us to establish His Kingdom on the earth in love and humility. Selfish ambition will eat away at the heart of the church. The first beatitude in Matthew is "Blessed are the poor in spirit" because those are the ones who are desperate for Jesus.

In meekness and humility, you consider others to be better than yourself. You never exalt yourself above others. If we claim to be Christian, then we must follow Jesus: "Your attitude should be the same as that of Christ Jesus: Who, being in very nature God, did not consider equality with God something to be grasped, but made Himself nothing, taking the very nature of a servant, being made in human likeness. And being found in appearance as a man, He humbled Himself and became obedient to death-- even death on a cross!" Philippians 2:5-8 (NIV)

In her book *Compelled by Love*, Heidi Baker says: "One of my favorite heroes in the faith is Mama Tanweke. She has raised three people from the dead, and together with Papa Tanweke, she oversees a region in our movement. Everywhere they preach, great signs and wonders follow. But she failed the third year of our Bible college! At graduation, the missionaries told me that she had failed the final exams because she could not read well enough.

Think about that: three people were raised from the dead, but she is a Bible school failure. Perhaps God does not care as much about our so-called ministry qualifications as we do! Mama Tanweke is just one of the meek ones who have inherited the earth in God's upside-down economy."

DAY 28

> "And so a whole nation came from this one man who was as good as dead—a nation with so many people that, like the stars in the sky and the sand on the seashore, there is no way to count them. All these people died still believing what God had promised them. They did not receive what was promised, but they saw it all from a distance and welcomed it." Hebrews 11:12-13 (NLT)

E dward Kimball was determined to win his Sunday school class to Christ. A teenager named Dwight Moody tended to fall asleep on Sundays, but Kimball, undeterred, set out to reach him at work. His heart was pounding as he entered the store where the young man worked. "I put my hand on his shoulder, and as I leaned over, I placed my foot upon a shoebox. I asked him to come to Christ." But Kimball left thinking he had botched the job. Moody, however, left the store that day a new person and eventually became the most prominent evangelist in America.

On June 17, 1873 Moody arrived in Liverpool, England for a series of crusades. The meetings went poorly at first but then the dam burst and blessing began flowing. Moody visited a Baptist chapel pastored by a scholarly man named F. B. Meyer, who at first disdained the American's unlettered (Moody had no Seminary degree) preaching. But Meyer was soon transfixed and transformed by Moody's message.

At Moody's invitation, Meyer toured America. At Northfield Bible Conference, he challenged the crowds saying, "If you are not willing to give up everything for Christ, are you willing to be made willing?" That remark changed the life of a struggling young minister named J. Wilber Chapman.

Chapman proceeded to become a powerful traveling evangelist in the early 1900s, and he recruited a converted baseball player named Billy Sunday. Under Chapman's eye, Sunday became one of the most spectacular evangelists in American history. His campaign in Charlotte, North Carolina, produced a group of converts who continued praying for another such visitation of the Spirit. In 1934 they invited evangelist Mordecai Ham to conduct a citywide crusade. On October 8th Ham, discouraged, wrote a prayer to God on the stationary of his Charlotte hotel: "Lord, give us a Pentecost here. . . Pour out Thy Spirit tomorrow. . ."

His prayer was answered beyond his dreams when a Central High School student named Billy Graham gave his heart to Jesus. Don't underestimate what God can do through you.

DAY 29

> "Finally, Abraham said, 'Lord, please don't be angry with me if I speak one more time. Suppose only ten are found there?' And the Lord replied, 'Then I will not destroy it for the sake of the ten.'"
> Genesis 18:32 (NLT)

Sometimes questions are seen as rebellion. I grew up in a church that discouraged questions. No one asked: "Why do we do Sunday school? Why do people have to dress up, or be quiet?" Questions are often discouraged because those in charge are unsure of the answers. "Because we've always done it that way" or "you just need to believe" are not real and authentic answers.

I need explanations; they don't have to be agreeable or likeable; just authentic and real. After all, God has a history of people who questioned Him and got away with it. Abraham bargained with God, Jacob wrestled, Mary questioned, Zechariah asked the same question—but as a priest was more accountable—yet his spanking was light: just a few months without speech. Job was commended by God in the end.

There is a difference between questions that seek to understand, and questions that are a result of cynicism.

God has just told Abraham He's about to check out Sodom and see how bad it is. He asks God if He'll destroy the city if He can find fifty righteous people there; then proceeds to barter God all the way down to ten.

Abraham is just trying to understand God. "Will You destroy the righteous with the wicked?" He's not accusing God; he's just trying to know Him better.

God wants us to press in to know Him better. And if by some chance we cross a line with our questions, God may decide to shut us up for a bit. But in the end, knowing how we can be, that's probably not such a bad idea anyway.

DAY 30

"For by the grace given me I say to every one of you: Do not think of yourself more highly than you ought, but rather think of yourself with sober judgment, in accordance with the measure of faith God has given you." Romans 12:3 (NIV)

To all the nobodies in the world: I'm with you. Wanting to be a somebody in this world won't cost you the Kingdom, but it may cost you a certain standing in the Kingdom and surely may disqualify you for certain rewards in the afterlife.

I had once mentioned something similar to this to a group of people and was answered with some pushback. "How can you say that there will be favoritism in Heaven?" someone asked. They went on to say, "that just doesn't seem fair." I could see their concern was as if I had said that only purple people go to Heaven.

My understanding is this: by the time we get into the afterlife, past the welcomes and the judgments of the wicked and whatever else may take place, we will be totally transformed. Paul said it happens so quick it is "in the blink of an eye" according to 1 Corinthians 15.

And in this transformed state it won't matter who gets what and when. In fact, we will be so different that we will celebrate everyone who gets rewarded, everyone who is lauded, everyone who seems special.

We will altogether at once understand that we are all nobodies and that Jesus is the only Somebody who ever lived. We won't be stung by our petty jealousies and our wounded egos. We won't have our rejected hearts slithering along on the ground waiting for someone to have pity on us and love us properly. We will have no desire greater than lifting up others around us, rejoicing that we even get to participate in this great dance of life and freedom. We will finally, truly, be free. Doesn't that sound like paradise to you?

DAY 31

"For everything that was written in the past was written to teach us, so that through endurance and the encouragement of the Scriptures we might have hope." Romans 15:4 (NIV)

L et's not be too quick to despair because the world seems to be darkening. Into a seemingly dark and despairing time, God choose to send His Son and offer salvation not only to those in that time—but to us as well. In the midst of a great darkness, God choose to shine His brightest light!

We've all had times or seasons in our lives where the heavens seemed like brass; as if our prayers stopped at the ceiling, or worse, just drooled off our lips and dripped to the ground. We've experienced darkness in our lives when it seemed that God was nowhere to be found; when the deepest cries of our hearts have gone unanswered— when we wished that just one thing in our lives would work out right.

Today, for those who are experiencing a time of despair—God offers you hope. I am not saying God will instantly remove all the negative circumstances of your life—but He offers you His presence. The Scriptures testify of God's faithfulness and goodness. The Messiah has come, the Holy Spirit is here to comfort, guide and to give life. Even if the world has failed you, or worse, the church has failed you—perhaps even your friends or family have failed you; God will not fail you. He is faithful. He will bring light to the darkest night. His timing is perfect. After a very long dry time of not hearing from the Lord—He will surprise us with His coming. The Bible is the testimony of God's faithfulness through all generations.

DAY 32

"For it is written: 'Be holy, because I am holy.'" 1 Peter 1:16 (NIV)

G od is holy. The result of our sin is that our relationship with Him is broken. God can't look at sin or have it in His presence. He loves us, but He can't embrace us as long as we embrace sin. We deserve to be punished by God for our rebellion. We have a problem that we cannot, on our own, make right.

I watched the TV in horror as the space shuttle exploded in a million tiny pieces, killing everyone on board. The ground crew knew that during lift-off, some small piece of the spacecraft broke off, but it didn't seem like a big deal at the time. But it was a big deal. It was a matter of life and death. That is how sin is in our lives.

A vaccination works by giving a person a small dose of the virus so that the body builds up its own immunity. As we have slowly indulged more and more in sin, we have become immune to its effects; we see it and think it's no big deal. But it is a big deal. Like the small piece of spacecraft that broke off, our sin is a matter of life and death.

God hates our sin and has great love for us. Both are true. God doesn't stop hating our sin in order to love us—it's not in His nature. He had to fix the sin problem in order to embrace us. Instead of punishing us for our sin, Jesus was punished. He went to the cross to demonstrate the love of God and satisfy God's holiness. That's how God made our problem right. Not by punishing us, but by sacrificing Himself.

DAY 33

"For the Son of Man came to seek and to save that which was lost." Luke 19:10 (ASV)

P hil Littleford took his son on an Alaskan fishing trip with two other men. In a quest to find some running salmon, they flew their seaplane to a secluded bay. The fishing was awesome. When they finished the day, the receding tide had left their plane on dry ground, twenty-three feet from the water. They cooked some fish for dinner and slept in the plane. When they awoke, the tide was in and their plane was drifting in the water. They cranked the engine and took off. Unknown to them, one of the pontoons had been punctured and was filled with water, causing the seaplane to crash within moments. Everyone survived, but without safety equipment, they had to use their waders as floating devices. The frigid water was a deadly threat. The current was too strong for Dr. Littleford's twelve-year-old son. The other two men fought their way against the tide and barely made it to shore. They looked back from shore to see Dr. Littleford and his son Mark being swept out to sea, arm-in-arm. The Coast Guard reported that they probably lasted no more than an hour in the freezing waters. The hypothermia chilled their bodies and put them to sleep. Mark, with a smaller body mass would fall asleep first and die in his father's arms. Dr. Littleford could have made it to shore, but that would have meant losing his son.

The term 'lost' describes the depth of God's love for us. Rick Warren says, "Our value is communicated by the word lost...things of value are lost, not misplaced. Jesus came to save the lost—showing us His incredible love by giving His life for ours!"

DAY 34

"For the wages of sin is death, but the gift of God is eternal life in Christ Jesus our Lord." Romans 6:23 (NIV)

T here seems to be a payoff for nearly everything. The payoff for eating lots of junk food full of fats and sugars is heart disease and diabetes. If you drive too fast and recklessly, you will be paid in an accident. The reward for a life of crime is prison or worse. In the animal kingdom, the payment for weakness is death.

And there is a positive side to wages—a worker gets money for labor; victory is often the return for intense competition. The diligent student is often rewarded with good grades.

Paul tells us in Romans that the payoff for sin is death. You sew sin; you reap death. It is stated as a fact, not an opinion. If one chooses to live enslaved to sin, they are choosing spiritual death which is separation from God forever.

But Paul goes further. Notice what he doesn't say. He doesn't say that the wages of a sinless life is eternal life with God. He makes it plain here, as well as in other places in Scripture, that eternal life cannot be earned. It is a gift that is given by God. It is not a reward for moral living; it is not a reward for the lack of sin in a person's life. Eternal life is a gift. Period.

But our gift cost Jesus dearly. Thank God that sin and death don't get the final word. Under God's grace, we don't get what we deserve. The wages of sin is death—but Jesus paid our debt. He died in our place so that we might live. That's why grace is so amazing.

DAY 35

"Then he said, "Your name shall no longer be Jacob, but Israel; for you have contended with God and with men, and have prevailed."
Genesis 32:28 (NASB)

G enesis records a wrestling match. It's not really a smack-down or even a caged match. God shows up and wrestles a man named Jacob.

Now Jacob has been self-defining his whole life. He has often taken things into his own hands to accomplish what he wanted. He stole his brothers' blessing, tricking and conning his way into it instead of waiting for God to give it to him. Jacob was always working an angle; always defending and protecting himself, trusting no one, always fighting his own battles.

But now we see Jacob is in a fight he cannot win. He wrestles with God all night and is unable to gain any ground. But he doesn't quit; he won't give up. And then God gives him a painful lesson.

While Jacob is holding his ground, God, with a single touch, throws Jacob's hip out of joint. Jacob the wrestler is now Jacob the clinger. He is holding on to God. This is a redefining moment for Jacob—he has never really lost before, at least, not like this. He has always been able to rely on his own strength or cunning or fortitude. But now he has lost control. He no longer has the high ground. Now everything has changed.

Jacob hangs on to God and says he won't let go until God blesses him. He may have been somewhat smug before, but he is smart enough to know when he is beaten. He will limp with the reminder of this encounter for the rest of his life.

God isn't offended by our wrestling with Him. And He doesn't wrestle us just to win; He wasn't bullying Jacob. He wrestles to show us a little more of who we are, and, in the process, a lot more of who He is. And in the end, Jacob's limp was a lifelong reminder of both.

DAY 36

> "We must keep our eyes on Jesus, who leads us and makes our faith complete. He endured the shame of being nailed to a cross, because he knew later on he would be glad he did. Now he is seated at the right side of God's throne!" Hebrews 12:2 (CEV)

G od responds to sin in the believer in three distinct ways: He justifies—that is, He removes the guilt and penalty of sin and imparts righteousness in Jesus. Secondly, He sanctifies—He breaks the power of our indwelling sin nature, enabling us to live a life pleasing to God. That indwelling sin nature is like a 'sin factory' that keeps producing sin. This process is enabled by a believer yielding himself to the Holy Spirit. Lastly, He glorifies—this is our transformation at the time of death.

So, what exactly happens in sanctification? When you become a Christian, Paul says 'you are dead to sin and alive to Christ.' Dead here does not mean 'annihilated' but simply separated. Your 'sin factory' is still able to operate, and you still have access to it, but it doesn't run you. Before your life in Christ, you could not separate yourself from your sin. Now in Christ, you can be free from sin's dominion over you.

People often ask, "If God has forgiven all my sin—then why do I have to ask for forgiveness?" 1 John 1:9 says that if we confess our sins, He forgives them and cleanses us from everything we've done wrong. John never says our eternal life with God is at jeopardy—that has been accomplished by faith. Once we become children of God we cannot be disowned. But continued sin will cloud our familial relations with God—we won't be in sync with Him. It's like we are still in the family, but we're just not talking.

Jesus died so we can have relationship with Him now—in fact, Jesus is eternal life. Jesus died so that our sin doesn't have to be our focus— our focus can be on Him!

DAY 37

"For you were bought at a price; therefore glorify God in your body and in your spirit, which are God's." 1 Corinthians 6:20 (NKJV)

God wants not so much things from us as He wants us. It is about a relationship with Him. To prepare a place for Him means that we must die to ourselves in order to make room for Him inside us. He won't compete with our selfishness and our self-rule. That was the mistake of our first parents— "not your will God, but ours be done".

"But what about me?" you might ask. "What will be left of me?" We've been repeatedly sold on the idea that we are the "masters of our own destiny," and much of this is coming from Christian circles.

The reality is that we were bought with a price. We belong to God. The answer to "what will be left of me?" is "not much." Oh, how that grates on our flesh! We've been told how special we are, and how much God loves us so that we don't even have to change!

But that's not it. Our old selves must die so that we can be transformed into sons and daughters. I don't mean that all of us are called to be martyrs like the Apostles, or even martyrs like Stephen. For some Christians, their lives will exhibit the qualities of fulfilling vocations and plenty of play time. It all comes from God. Lewis says that "in a perfect Christian they would be as much part of his "Christianity" as his hardest duties, and his feasts would be as Christian as his fasts."

There is no place in our life that Christ does not take claim over. He is our life; our life is no longer our own. Just as the Bible teaches us; we must die to live. Only then will we become our truest selves.

Heavenly Father, may I surrender all that I really am, to all that You are. I choose You, Lord, the only one who satisfies.

DAY 38

G od has so much to say about us in the Bible—and yet people seem to get their information from every other source. The reality is that if we don't understand who we are from God, then we are allowing the enemy, or the world, to define us.

If we continue to believe the lies of the enemy, we will eventually develop the symptoms. These symptoms include a horrible view of ourselves and an impotence in living the Christian life.

There was a wealthy New York woman who invited friends over for a banquet. The cook called her in to the kitchen to ask her about some mushrooms that had been delivered that could be toadstools. The woman suggested giving them to an old dog. After a while, the dog seemed fine, so they went ahead and fed their guests. Suddenly, the cook ran in to tell the woman that the old dog had died. She told everyone the entire story, and suddenly all her guests got sick and they called for ambulances. But the woman was confused because she had no symptoms. She decided to go and check on the old dog, but the cook said, "You don't want to see him now, he's quite a mess after getting hit by that truck."

The enemy tells us lies; he whispers to us in the dark that God doesn't love us, won't take care of us, and is never pleased with us. It is important—no, it is necessary for us to go and "check on the old dog" like the woman in the story—we need to get at the truth. Don't settle for the thoughts that rattle around in your head—take the truth of God's word to heal your life.

God is calling for change. We need to become a new kind of people who ask the really tough questions: Where has God's glory gone from the church? When did the church become a "bless me" club rather than a "laying everything down for the sake of Christ" fellowship? When did we change from dying to ourselves, taking up our cross and following Jesus into the gospel of "me", "my", and "mine?" When did it become more important to be concerned about how we look than who we really are when no one is looking?

DAY 39

G od often takes longer than we expect. Judging by the way some of us pray, you'd think God was a cosmic bellhop just waiting for us to ring our bell so He could grab our bags and show us our room. We are so disappointed when we ring and He doesn't show up.

Abraham and Sarah experienced long waits, as did Moses, and Hannah, and most of the prophets. God often takes the long walk. For Him a thousand years are as a day and a day is as a thousand years. As one author put it: "With God, timing is more important than time."

And yet we have the prayer of the persistent widow in Luke 18. The passage begins with these words, "Then Jesus told His disciples a parable to show them that they should always pray and not give up." Now I'm thinking that is not really good news. What I read in a statement like that is, "God may take a really long time in answering your prayer, so I need to teach you not to give up." Why, you might ask, do we need to be taught not to give up? Because you are going to feel like giving up.

In Luke 11 the disciples ask Jesus to teach them to pray and He tells them a story about a friend who needs bread at midnight because someone has shown up and they've got nothing to feed them. The moral of the story is "Ask and keep asking and you'll finally get what you're asking for".

Eventually.

What all these stories have in common is relationship—at least if we are persistent in our prayers, we are still talking to God. And that seems to be what He is most interested in.

"The Lord is not slow in keeping his promise, as some understand slowness. Instead he is patient with you, not wanting anyone to perish, but everyone to come to repentance." 2 Peter 3:9 (NIV)

DAY 40

"God loved the world so much that He gave His one and only Son so that whoever believes in Him may not be lost, but have eternal life." John 3:16 (NCV)

U pon becoming a Christian, significant transformations occur in both the heavenly and earthly realms. Initially, you might only be able to articulate that you acknowledge Jesus Christ of Scripture as your Savior and Lord.

Soon after, you'll notice you've been transformed. Both demonic and angelic beings have recognized you as someone fundamentally changed. A supernatural element now exists in your life that wasn't there before.

Your position before God has also shifted. He now views you through the perspective of His Son Jesus. Your sins are completely covered by the blood Jesus poured out at the cross. You're no longer subject to God's condemnation. He regards you as He regards His Son. This doesn't mean He's unaware of reality, but rather He deliberately chooses to see you as ransomed. He has bought you back; you no longer are your own possession, nor do you belong to the world or the devil. You are God's. You'll start to find sin less appealing and discover a fresh desire to honor God.

Not only have you been spiritually reborn to dwell with God eternally, but you've also joined God's family. You may discover that some fellow believers are foolish, irresponsible, uninteresting, or insincere. However, we're all growing; we're all traveling this path together. Keep in mind that God loves them even when you struggle to. Simply treat them as you'd hope to be treated yourself.

Lastly, understand that you're now opposed by hell, its dark armies, and Satan himself. Yet you needn't live in terror—the God dwelling within you intimidates and discourages them. Given the opportunity, they'll attempt to tempt you. They'll resist you. If you remain casual and careless in your walk with Jesus, expect little interference from them. But embrace your dedication to Christ wholeheartedly and they'll battle you fiercely. Nevertheless, our victory comes through Jesus, the sovereign King over all.

DAY 41

"So the last will be first, and the first will be last." Matthew 20:16
(NIV)

G od's value system is different from ours. For us the words "good" and "blessing" signify comfort and convenience and happy circumstances. But to God the same words may signify character and virtue and integrity. We think in physical and material terms; God thinks in spiritual terms. To Him, holiness is better than happiness, character more desirable than comfort.

When Jesus came on the scene, He announced a Kingdom that seemed completely upside down from the normal world. When the world said, "The best will be first," He said, "The first will be last." When the world said, "Do to others before they do to you," He said, "Treat others as you'd like to be treated." When the world said, "Live for yourself," He said, "Die to yourself in order to live."

This was an other-worldly Kingdom. It was not over in this province or in that region. It was not a tribe of people whom He would lead to overthrow the Roman occupiers. The Kingdom of God was the rule and reign of the King—Jesus Christ. Wherever God's desires were made manifest—where there were people putting their faith in Jesus, being healed from sickness, delivered from demons, set free from sin and addictions, and raised from the dead—that was the Kingdom!

Jesus asked His followers to pray to the Father, "Your Kingdom come, Your will be done on earth as it is in Heaven." This is not a prayer for a better society or for more comfort and peace on earth. This is a radical request for the invasion of this world by the Architect of Society and the Prince of Peace Himself. It's not like anything you'd expect. It can take your breath away. This is no ordinary Kingdom.

DAY 42

"He replied, 'If you have faith as small as a mustard seed, you can say to this mulberry tree, "Be uprooted and planted in the sea," and it will obey you.'" Luke 17:6 (NIV)

S aving faith needs to grow in us. But not in the way a seed grows to maturity. Faith must take root in our hearts—we must grow in our ability to let faith really grab us. It is never a question of how large or how mature our faith is; it is a question of having it or not.

I am talking about saving faith—not just mental assent. James 2:19 says, "You believe that there is one God. Good! Even the demons believe that-- and shudder." So even demons believe; but it is not a faith that saves them.

The Great Blondin stretched a tightrope across Niagara Falls and asked a visiting official if he believed he could carry someone across the falls in a wheelbarrow. The official said "yes," at which Blondin replied, "Get in."

Saving faith has action; it is either or—either you believe and would stake your life on it or you don't. Jesus talked about other kinds of faith—like when the disciples were afraid because of the storm—and said "oh you little faiths!" as a rebuke. But saving faith is either or; you cannot have just a little.

So, if someone says, "you don't measure up" you say, "yes, you are right— thank God that Jesus has measured up for me." Saving faith is getting in the wheelbarrow; it is staking our life on a faith that says that if Jesus doesn't save me, I am forever, eternally lost because I cannot save myself. That's saving faith.

DAY 43

Hebrews 3:18-19 (NLT) says, "And to whom was God speaking when He took an oath that they would never enter His rest? Wasn't it the people who disobeyed Him? So we see that because of their unbelief they were not able to enter His rest."

The children of Israel were unable to enter into God's rest because of their unbelief; but what was it they were unable to believe? Oswald Chambers said, "The root of all sin is the suspicion that God is not good."

Hebrews says that Israel had been deceived by sin and their hearts had become hard. They stopped believing the best about God. They tested Him—resisted Him all along the way. They complained about their deliverance out of Egypt saying, "if only the Lord had killed us back in Egypt." They whined about their thirst, grumbled about manna, and then rebelled against Moses and the Promised Land.

But we're not so different; we can find ourselves resisting God all along the way. We pray for help and then complain when it does not come fast enough. We whine if it's not the kind of help we wanted. We accuse God of not caring.

Then we find ourselves worn out. We are tired. We can't get enough rest. There is too much to do and never enough time to do it.

But that is what the writer of Hebrews is saying. We can't enter God's rest if we resist Him; we can't rest if we don't believe He is good and is committed to our care and well-being. Rebellion against God will leave us weak and tired—unable to get the nourishment we need to live. The work God wants from us is to believe in the one He has sent.

DAY 44

"For in hope we have been saved, but hope that is seen is not hope; for who hopes for what he already sees?" Romans 8:24 (NASB)

H ope is a powerful force that has the ability to inspire, motivate, and uplift individuals in times of adversity. One true historical event that embodies the essence of hope is the story of Anne Frank during the Holocaust.

Anne Frank was a young Jewish girl who, along with her family, went into hiding in Amsterdam in an attempt to escape the atrocities of the Nazi regime during World War II. Despite the unimaginable challenges and dangers they faced, Anne held onto hope and documented her experiences and innermost thoughts in her now- famous diary. Through her words, we see the resilience and courage of a young girl who refused to let despair consume her.

In the midst of darkness and despair, Anne found solace in writing and dreaming of a better future. Her faith in God held her strong. Her unwavering hope kept her going, despite the constant fear and uncertainty that surrounded her. In one of her entries, Anne wrote, "I don't think of all the misery but of the beauty that still remains." God gave this young woman the ability to find light in the midst of darkness, to hold onto hope even in the bleakest of circumstances.

Anne's story serves as a reminder that hope is not always born out of ideal circumstances, but rather out of the grace of God to endure and overcome. Despite the horrors of the Holocaust, Anne never gave up on the belief that a better tomorrow was possible. Her resilience, optimism, and unwavering faith in God continue to inspire generations of people around the world.

Anne's legacy lives on not only through her diary but also through the millions of lives she has touched with her story of hope and resilience. Her unwavering belief in the power of God serves as a beacon of light in times of darkness, reminding us that even in the face of unimaginable hardship, there is always reason to hope.

The story of Anne Frank during the Holocaust is a powerful reminder of the enduring power of hope. Through her words and her spirit, Anne exemplified the strength and resilience that comes from holding onto hope in the face of adversity. Her story is a testament to the greatness of God and a reminder that hope has the power to transcend even the darkest of times.

DAY 45

Haratio Spafford wrote the hymn "It is Well With My Soul." He had known peaceful and happy days as a successful attorney in Chicago. He was the father of five children, an active member of the Presbyterian Church, and a loyal friend and supporter of D. L. Moody and other evangelical leaders of his day. Without warning, a series of unexpected events occurred. First, there was the sudden death of the Spafford's only son. Then, a short time later, the great Chicago fire wiped out the family's extensive real estate investments. Spafford decided to take his family to Europe, to help out in Moody's evangelistic campaign there.

In November 1873, Spafford was detained by urgent business, but sent his wife and four daughters as scheduled on the S. S. du Harve, planning to join them soon. Halfway across the Atlantic, the ship was struck by an English vessel and sank in 12 minutes. All four of the Spafford daughters were among the 226 that drowned. Mrs. Spafford was among the few who were miraculously saved.

Haratio Spafford stood hour after hour on the deck of the ship carrying him to rejoin his sorrowing wife in Wales. When the ship passed the approximate place where his precious daughters had drowned, Spafford received sustaining comfort from God that enabled him to write: "When peace like a river attendeth my way, when sorrows like sea billows roll, whatever my lot Thou hast taught me to say, it is well it is well with my soul. My sin oh the joy of this glorious thought, my sin not in part but the whole, is nailed to the cross and I bear it no more, praise the Lord, praise the Lord O my soul." Only God can give such peace.

"Peace I leave with you; my peace I give you. I do not give to you as the world gives. Do not let your hearts be troubled and do not be afraid." John 14:27 (NIV)

DAY 46

How can we humans have an encounter with a spirit-God who is both invisible and holy? We cannot see something or someone who is spirit. And the sight of His perfection—His holiness—would kill us.

Even so God, who is always more ready to draw near to us than we to Him, can and does reveal Himself in symbolic forms. Some are simple and easy to understand and others are baffling and complex. But whatever the symbolic form, or however obscure, the impact on the individual is always overwhelming.

Pascal claims to have had such an experience with the Lord. Scholars are both frustrated and intrigued by his sparse details of the event. With mathematical precision he records not only the date, but the precise times of its beginning and end. Except for the content of the encounter, he leaves us one word only— "FIRE."

Others have commonly described themselves as weeping, as feeling a loss of strength, as trembling, as experiencing a strange combination of joy and terror. When the utter holiness of God is in view, people often suffer from an appalling sense of their own wretchedness and of their own sin.

At other times, God grants us experiences of Himself that overwhelm us with His love, joy and peace. Although our perceptions are feeble compared to the blazing reality that nearly knocks us out, we sense that this love, joy and peace are eternal reality.

Other experiences are far more ordinary, yet the Lord is in them as well. He knows what we need. Sometimes He will stretch our faith by not showing Himself at all. The real miracle is that He cares enough to tailor each of our spiritual journeys in the way that we need in order to draw us closer to Himself.

DAY 47

I am not suggesting this, but if you were to take a mild tranquilizer half an hour before a family meltdown, you would probably convey great peace when it happened. Your anxiety would lessen and you might float through the whole thing calm and gentle. Conflict in the family would seem like no big deal, and you could approach problems calmly as long as the effects of the pill lasted. Perhaps your serenity would spread to other family members as well—but at the cost of exposing you to a bad and dangerous habit.

I am not recommending tranquilizers for family problems. What we really need is a genuine peace—the kind that'll make a dog wag his tail and babies hold out their arms to you. Neither am I recommending a casual peace of "oh it doesn't really matter," a so-called peace that lets important matters slide or that fails to come to grips with real problems. The peace I am talking about must not condone irresponsibility or escapism; but must arise from an inner assurance that all is well—the clear-eyed peace of a person who is in touch with God.

When you are upset, irritated and angry, you cannot contribute to peace in others. But when your spirit is quiet and at rest, then when you intervene in a fight your peace will reassure others, diminishing their resentment. Move in with aggression and you may gain some control over others, but you will never solve the resentments and bitterness that gave rise to the explosion in the first place. A gentle and quiet spirit is of great price in God's sight and an equally priceless resource in family life. Proverbs 15:1 says, "A gentle answer deflects anger, but harsh words make tempers flare."

DAY 48

I believe that God heals today. But in the end, there are no cures, only postponements. The Scriptures say, "And as it is appointed unto men once to die, but after this the judgment." Unless Jesus returns again in our lifetime, everyone must face death. I have been dying since the day I was born, but no one has really prepared me for death.

There are no cures, only postponements. The shadow of death looms over us—real and inevitable. But we don't talk about it. Our society, like many throughout history, reveres youth and despises the old. We hide the elderly in institutions. Our mortality is out of sight and out of mind.

We say the dead have "passed away," or "passed on." Elisabeth Kubler-Ross tells of the time she approached the head of a six-hundred-bed facility and said, "I'd like to work with some dying people." The administrator said, "In our hospital, nobody dies. They expire." Our death-denial produces a heightened fear of death in many people.

Yet we should never give up hope for healing or take that hope away from the sick. We should keep praying for healing as long as we can. But when it becomes obvious that the person is going to die, we have a greater duty to help them die in dignity and peace.

We don't have to fight death—Christ has fought and won. In Philippians Paul writes: "I'm torn between two desires: Sometimes I want to live, and sometimes I long to go and be with Christ. That would be far better for me." Death for the believer is to be present with the Lord. Death means going to be with Jesus. He is eternal life!

Let us therefore walk with integrity, living in the tension between a God who heals, while living in a body that is not meant to live forever.

DAY 49

"Not only that, but we also boast in our sufferings, knowing that suffering produces endurance, endurance produces character, and character produces hope." Romans 5:3-4 (ISV)

I have been told that experienced mountaineers have a quiet, regular, short step as they climb. It doesn't look like much, but they plod along steadily, on and on they ascend, while the novice climber hurries along, and soon has to stop unable to go further. And when expert mountaineers encounter thick mists along the journey, they halt and camp out under some slight cover brought with them, moving on only when the mist has cleared away.

Now if you want to grow in virtue, to serve God, and to love Christ, you will grow in and attain to these things if you will take them with a slow and sure mountain plod. You must make a quiet steady ascent, willing to have to camp for weeks or months in spiritual desolation, darkness and emptiness at different stages in your march and growth. All demand for constant light, or comfort should be avoided. Any attempt at eliminating or minimizing the cross and trial, will, in the long run, only slow your progress and weaken your resolve.

Contrary to what might be expected, I look back on experiences that at the time seemed especially desolating and painful with satisfaction. I can say with complete truthfulness that everything I have learned in my sixty-eight years in this world, everything that has truly enhanced and enlightened my life, has been through affliction and not through happiness. I believe that if it were possible to eliminate hardship from our lives by means of some drug or magic, the result would not make life more enjoyable, but it would make it too dull and trivial to be endured. This is what the Cross signifies. Jesus today has many who love His heavenly Kingdom, but few who carry His cross.

DAY 50

"I want to know Christ—yes, to know the power of His resurrection and participation in His sufferings, becoming like Him in His death." Philippians 3:10

S ometimes our expectations get in the way of what God is doing. We often expect that our experience of God will be perfect. But there is no such thing as a perfect revival. Even on the day of Pentecost— men under the power of God's Spirit were accused of being drunk.

The problem is not God, it's us. God is pure, but we're not. God's judgments are true, but ours can be off. So, we should be careful with our critique lest we offend the Holy Spirit. The Pharisees accused Jesus of working through the devil's power. Gamaliel, in Acts five, speaking of the Apostles, says: "And so now I tell you: stay away from these men and leave them alone. If their plan comes from human authority, it will fail. But if it is from God, you will not be able to stop them. You might even be fighting against God Himself." We see through a glass dimly.

Yet Jesus says that we can trust the Father to give us good gifts if we ask. It all boils down to trusting God. Long ago Jonathan Edwards put it this way: "Those that are critical of the present work of God among us have gone about it the wrong way. In judging whether or not this is from God, they have judged the means and the methods; but it is not the means and the methods that tell us if this is from God—it is the fruit of it."

In other words, it doesn't matter what you experience—whether you flip, float or fly. If it doesn't make you more in love with Jesus—with more devotion to His Word, His people and His cause, then, in the end, all you have had is an experience. Remember, encountering God on a personal level is always an experience, but we never seek God to get something from Him, we seek Him to know Him better.

DAY 51

I was watching a TV show the other night, and a policeman who had committed a crime was arrested and took his own life in his jail cell. Just before being locked up, he told the lead detective, "Everyone must pay for their mistakes."

Did you ever wonder where our sense of justice came from? What tells us that one thing is worse than another—or what compels us to believe that people should pay for their mistakes?

Of course, there are times when we wish we had a 'get out of jail free' card. But even when we think that, aren't we saying it takes a special card, a special grace, to let us off the hook? We still believe that we are guilty—we don't deny the guilt, we just desire mercy over judgment, especially for ourselves.

Christianity doesn't say we are not guilty. It doesn't say our guilt does not matter. In fact, it says the opposite. It not only states that we are guilty, but that in the midst of how badly we treat each other, God is the party chiefly offended. And it goes further, saying that we are helpless, in an of ourselves, to rectify the situation.

So, God in His mercy has done for us what we could not do for ourselves. Jesus came to pay for our failures. There is no dungeon so dark, no sin so great, that the light of God's love in Jesus cannot find us. Left to ourselves, all we have is our guilt and sin with no remedy.

But God has not left us to ourselves; in His great love, He has removed the barrier of sin between us and offered us a life of freedom—Jesus paid it all.

"Christ died once for our sins. An innocent person died for those who are guilty. Christ did this to bring you to God, when his body was put to death and his spirit was made alive." 1 Peter 3:18
(CEV)

DAY 52

I wish you could see death the way I see it. I've done so many funerals over the years that I've lost count, and I can't tell you the number of funerals I have done for people whose life seems to have been cut short.

The veil between this life and the next sometimes seems paper thin and fragile. Even though we push it out of our thoughts until some illness or tragedy grips us, death is ever at our doorstep. You were born dying. You just never expect to go to bed one evening knowing that this will be your last night on earth. It is a sobering thought. Jesus addresses this in Luke 16:19-31.

"There was a rich man who was dressed in purple and fine linen and lived in luxury every day. At his gate was laid a beggar named Lazarus, covered with sores and longing to eat what fell from the rich man's table. Even the dogs came and licked his sores. The time came when the beggar died and the angels carried him to Abraham's side. The rich man also died and was buried. In hell, where he was in torment, he looked up and saw Abraham far away, with Lazarus by his side. So, he called to him,

'Father Abraham, have pity on me and send Lazarus to dip the tip of his finger in water and cool my tongue, because I am in agony in this fire.'

But Abraham replied, 'Son, remember that in your lifetime you received your good things, while Lazarus received bad things, but now he is comforted here and you are in agony. And besides all this, between us and you a great chasm has been fixed, so that those who want to go from here to you cannot, nor can anyone cross over from there to us.'

He answered, 'Then I beg you, father, send Lazarus to my father's house, for I have five brothers. Let him warn them, so that they will not also come to this place of torment.'"

Reflective Meditation

"Even though I walk through the valley of the shadow of death, I will fear no evil, for You are with me" (Psalm 23:4). Rabbinical literature suggests that David was speaking of the wilderness of Ziph--one of the harshest seasons of his life. It was there he was hunted by Saul, betrayed by those he trusted, and pressed into deeper dependence on God's nearness. Yet even in that lonely and dangerous place he could say, I will not fear because the Lord was his constant companion.

"Your rod and Your staff, they comfort me". Again, in much of the Rabbinical teaching, the rod is seen as a symbol of the trials and hardships God allows to strengthen and refine His people, and the staff as a picture of Torah--God's instruction and guidance (the first five books of the Bible). Both, together, bring comfort. The people of Israel have long read this verse through the lens of their own suffering and the faithful light of Scripture, seeing in it a reminder that God is present not only in peace, but also in pain.

Another way to understand this passage comes from the life of a shepherd. The rod was used to protect sheep from predators and dangers. The staff was the tool of care--used to count the sheep, to examine when wounded or tangled, to guide them gently and even draw them back when they wandered. Both of these in the hands of a good shepherd who loves his sheep provided protection, guidance, strength and tenderness.

The "valley of the shadow of death" is not only a place of danger, it is any season in which we feel life pressed thin. Paul speaks of such a time in 2 Corinthians 2: 1:8-9:

"We were under great pressure, far beyond our ability to endure, so that we despaired of life itself. Indeed, we felt we had received the sentence of death. But this happened that we might not rely on ourselves but on God, who raised the dead."

When death, sorrow, fear or uncertainty draw near, the Shepherd draws nearer still. The Scriptures become our anchor, His presence our comfort, and His guidance our peace.

DAY 53

I would prefer not be accused as being a critic of the charismatic arm of the church; it is what I have lived in for many year. But I have seen the nastiness of non-charismatics (with whom I grew up with) who believe they have a special place with God because they have the best theology. That arrogance is identical to those who in the charismatic circles claim the high ground because they hear God more clearly than other peoples. Both are excessive and wrong.

I just can't find anywhere in Scripture an example of God being a daily manager over our lives, constantly speaking to us, directing us in every decision in every moment. And as I said earlier, and I'd like to reiterate, that would take responsibility completely away from us because everything we do is what God said to do.

Here is another problem that has caused this idea of a chatty God to arise. It is rooted in the idea that when the Holy Spirit does a work in a person, it is more like magic than not. It comes in subtly with statements like, "Jesus suffered for me so that I don't have to."

Jesus was made perfect in suffering, so you think you don't need it? And how about, "Jesus is the one who sanctifies, so I don't have to do anything myself." That is akin to a person saying, "well, if Jesus wants me to speak in tongues, He's gonna have move my lips and open my jaw." Those are terrible assumptions about how God works. If you are waiting for God to open your mouth and manipulate your tongue and vocal cords before you ever will speak in tongues, then chances are you will never speak in tongues. It is the same with our character formation—our best selves are formed in the fires of affliction. So don't run from It.

In the Bible there are always two sides— what God does and how we respond. Now I know some believe that it is all God, but I just don't see that played out in the Scripture. Why would Jesus stand up at a large gathering, and with a loud voice exclaim, "all who are thirsty come!", if He really meant "only those who are called should come." He means what He says. It is God's will that all should come to repentance, but God has allowed His will to be thwarted in this great enterprise. Not all will come, but God wills all to come.

DAY 54

"If a thing is free to be good it is also free to be bad. And free will is what has made evil possible. Why, then, did God give them free will? Because free will, though it makes evil possible, is also the only thing that makes possible any love or goodness or joy worth having." C. S. Lewis

C ould God create a world where creatures have free will, but never experience any negative consequences from their choices? And if there were no possible negative outcomes, would their choices truly count as free will in the first place?

Could God even create a world where creatures are given free will, but no one is allowed to murder, maim or even defame another creature? If that could be done, it would void the notion of free will.

To say that God is all-powerful and can do anything He wants is true— knowing that God doesn't involve Himself in nonsense. When I was in Bible College, someone asked "If God is so powerful, could He build a rock so big that He couldn't lift it?" But that is not a serious question, it is foolishness. God could not build a world that is intrinsically impossible—such as a world with free will but no negative consequences.

Human beings, being fallen from the grace of God in the Garden of Eden, seem incapable of taking responsibility for their own choices. It began early, as Adam complained to God regarding his own sin (found in Genesis 3), "And He said, 'Who told you that you were naked? Have you eaten from the tree that I commanded you not to eat from?' The man said, 'The woman you put here with me— she gave me some fruit from the tree, and I ate it.'" Ahh, so Adam blames Eve. But then, what does Eve do? She blames the devil. "Then the Lord God said to the woman, 'What is this you have done?' The woman said, 'The serpent deceived me, and I ate.'"

Free will is a double-edged sword. On the one hand, it is wonderful to be free, to be able to love, to enjoy life and fully live. On the other hand, being free means that you must choose to do good or evil. It is a grievous error to blame God or the devil for the evil that we do. God forgive us.

DAY 55

I f Christianity is real, then it should work (that is, true to its' purposes). Christianity is not just some philosophy or abstract set of ideas; it is a relationship with the living God. It is real and it works. But we must define what we mean when we say 'it works'. Do we mean it will make you popular and beautiful and everything will go your way? Do we mean that it will connect you with God so that you have all your prayers answered? What does it mean?

Jesus told the Apostle Paul: "'My grace is sufficient for you, for my power is made perfect in weakness.' Therefore, I will boast all the more gladly about my weaknesses, so that Christ's power may rest on me. That is why, for Christ's sake, I delight in weaknesses, in insults, in hardships, in persecutions, in difficulties. For when I am weak, then I am strong." 2 Corinthians 12:9-10 (NIV)

Or maybe when we say Christianity works, we mean that God's power working in us is what counts—that rather than being 'all that' we become nothing so that Christ power may rest on us. That is what Paul is saying. Jesus said it this way:

"If any of you wants to be my follower, you must turn from your selfish ways, take up your cross daily, and follow me." Luke 9:23 (NLT)

Brokenness is the knowledge that we need God. Brokenness is knowing that our self-sufficiency is poison to us. It is meekness; but meekness is not defined as mousiness or putting yourself down. Meekness means 'not fighting against God'. It means surrendering yourself to Him; picking up your cross. But we don't like brokenness; it is often despised as a weakness. We prefer to be self- contained and self-sufficient; but we must turn from them to follow Him.

DAY 56

"If I am delayed, you will know how people ought to conduct themselves in God's household, which is the church of the living God, the pillar and foundation of the truth." 1 Timothy 3:15 (NIV)

H ere the Apostle Paul is telling Timothy the reason for his letter— to instruct God's people how to be the church. The church is literally Christ's body on this earth, and as such, we are called to live responsibly before the watching world.

The New Testament teaches that a spiritual community is an alternative community—one in which the world can see that we actually believe in Jesus so much, that we've attributed so much intelligence to Him, so much worth, that we matter-of-factly order our lives around becoming like Him.

A spiritual community should be counter-cultural without being an escape from reality. Lives of sacrifice, humility, modesty, self- discipline, and preferring others are not considered normal in our society. But we must challenge the worldly norms around us, not by holding up signs that say, "God hates gays!", but with lives of such love and goodness that they defy understanding, and cause outsiders to ask, "what is it that causes you to live this way?"

Christianity spread so rapidly in the early years of the church not because they out-argued the pagans, but because they outloved them!

Their relationship to the world was not reactive, but proactive. They simply made Jesus their master and routinely gave to those who stole from them, loved those who mistreated them, blessed those who cursed them, lived humbly, and laid down their lives for others. They were the gospel in action—the gospel painted on the canvas of human lives. It was an irresistible force.

DAY 57

If the world is looking for something real, why do so many Christians seem to be faking it? Why do so many Christians hide behind a veneer of religious words and phrases? Why does their voice inflection change when they talk about 'God stuff' or church? Why do they act so uptight when people cuss, but seem perfectly at home when people gossip?

Brennan Manning says, "The Rabbi doesn't want us to be perfect, just real. Yet at times we try so hard to please God and impress others—determined to be perfect Christians—that we are sucked dry of energy and sickened by our own slick surface and inner hypocrisy...The Rabbi's heartbeat is for us, not against us. Though He will always cut away the counterfeit green and barrenness of our hypocrisy, He will never crush the bruised reed of our broken lives. The hewn branches He leaves along the pathway are never the result of disgust but always the result of His care-filled pruning."

We don't have anything to prove. As believers, God already loves and accepts us. And once that is established, we can accept the reality of our sinfulness; we can accept our real self. We no longer have to hide, play games, or run from reality.

God doesn't reveal our true condition to crush us, but to heal us. We can be at peace with God and man, not thinking more highly of ourselves than we ought, and not hating a part of ourselves. God breaks down the walls of division between us and Him; between each of us and even within ourselves. When Christ died to save us, He died to save every part of us; there is no place in us His love cannot reach.

DAY 58

"If we find ourselves with a desire that nothing in this world can satisfy, the most probable explanation is that we were made for another world." C.S. Lewis

O ne of the things that captured my imagination while reading Lewis was an intense desire for my own far-off country. In his children's series, "The Chronicles of Narnia," Narnia was a land entered by a special kind of wardrobe (in the beginning of the first book, and later by other means). It was a land of talking animals, strange by wonderful beings (like satyrs), and seemed like a unique land of magical wonder. At the center of it all was Aslan the lion, who turns out to be a type of Jesus from our world.

This longing shared by Lewis was infectious. While in college, there was a group of us who read the books simultaneously as if we had all stumbled upon some lost treasure. We were fascinated, and surprised, and simply blown away by the stories.

But the most infectious part was this awakening of a sense of longing in all of us. Some were even speculating (in a frivolous sort of way), that perhaps we could, under a waterfall, or even a special place in the woods, find a gateway into a magical world like Narnia.

We didn't realize it immediately, but this longing—for the beauty, the memories of our own past, and the desire for a special far-off country—are decent images of what we really desire, but if they are somehow are taking the place of the real object of our longing they are, in the end, just mute idols that cannot speak or hear. They are the roar of the ocean sans the salt, sand and sharks. They are the scent of a rose without the thorns. Instead, Lewis was sharing with us the ultimate object of all of our longing—to be with God Himself.

God is the source of these longings. He has put "eternity in our hearts," as someone once said. As a young man, Lewis believed that such feelings existed for their own sake, and one must pursue them hoping to end up with the genuine thing. However, Lewis later argued that these desires were seeded by God into our hearts to point us to His Son. Lewis says,

"Glory, as Christianity teaches me to hope for it, turns out to satisfy my original desire and indeed to reveal an element in that desire which I had not noticed. By ceasing for a moment to consider my own wants I have begun to learn better what I really wanted."

Our desires ultimately point us to the Father who accepts us in Christ. To be loved as God really loves us is the pinnacle of our longings, the genuine destination of our souls.

DAY 59

I f you consider yourself a leader in the church, are you willing to pay the price to lead? Have you ever thought about the fact that leading can be very difficult at times.

Dr. Evan O'Neill Kane made history twice in the same day. The chief surgeon of Kane Summit Hospital in NYC was convinced that local anesthesia was a better option than the accepted practice of always using general anesthesia. Dr. Kane felt the patient sustained too many risks when completely put under. His plan was to find a volunteer who would allow him to perform an appendectomy (an operation he had performed nearly four thousand times) with local anesthesia. The search was difficult because prospects feared the local deadening might wear off, leaving them in great pain. Others did not believe it would work. At last, Dr. Kane found a willing volunteer. On February 15, 1921 the volunteer was prepared for surgery and given local anesthesia. The sixty-year-old surgeon performed the procedure without any complications. Dr. Kane proved his point, as the patient experienced only minor discomfort. Naturally, Dr. Kane became famous as a surgeon that day, but even more interesting is the fact that he became famous for being the patient as well. He proved his theory by operating on himself! Leadership shines brightest when the leader does what nobody else is willing to do.

Too often the church has adopted abusive, Machiavellian principles of leadership; but not Jesus. In Mark 10 He says: "You know that those who are regarded as rulers of the Gentiles lord it over them, and their high officials exercise authority over them. Not so with you. Instead, whoever wants to become great among you must be your servant...For even the Son of Man did not come to be served, but to serve, and to give His life as a ransom for many." Real Christian leaders are always servants first.

He sat down, called the twelve disciples over to him, and said, "Whoever wants to be first must take last place and be the servant of everyone else." Mark 9:35 (NLT)

DAY 60

"If you forgive those who sin against you, your heavenly Father will forgive you. But if you refuse to forgive others, your Father will not forgive your sins." Matthew 6:14-15 (NLT)

W e are either in the hands of God or in the hands of people. If we are in the hands of people, we will spend our lives running from place to place because we weren't treated right, or were sinned against. But if we are in the hands of God, we don't have to run from people—we can respond to God rather than react to people.

People, even other Christians, will hurt us and sin against us from time to time. The question is not, 'will believers ever hurt me', it is, 'when I am hurt by a believer, will I be able to extend the same forgiveness that Jesus offered?'

Christians are called to forgive. Period. If we don't, we have a problem with our heavenly Father. Dr. John Ironside records this incident concerning Chiang Kai-shek at the time he was ruling mainland China:

"We all noticed a short time ago the account of the professed conversion of the President of China. We hope there has been a real work in his soul, but time will tell. I was reading how he came to his Christian wife who was saved long before he made a profession, and said, 'I can't understand these Christians; they have been treated most abominably here, they've been robbed, beaten, many of them killed; they have been persecuted fearfully; yet I never find one of them retaliating, and any time they can do something for China, for our people, they are ready to do it; I do not understand them.' 'Well,' said his wife, 'that, you see, is the very essence of Christianity. They do that because they are Christians.'"

That's what Christians do; they forgive not because people deserve it, but because they themselves have been forgiven.

DAY 61

"I'm not asking you to take them out of the world, but to keep them safe from the evil one. They do not belong to this world any more than I do. Make them holy by Your truth; teach them Your word, which is truth. Just as You sent me into the world, I am sending them into the world." John 17:15-18 (NLT)

I n the world, but not of the world. Throughout history the church has struggled to be in the world but not participating in the evil in the world.

The church finds itself embracing part of the culture, and resisting part of the culture. Within the church, there is disagreement about what part of the culture we should embrace and what part we should resist.

Do we participate in Christmas, or Halloween? Do we have TVs in our homes? Do we boycott movies? Should we stand outside the culture on these holidays? If we participate, how far should we go?

Part of the Church's answer has been to completely separate from the culture and live in closed, Christian communities. They take Paul's admonition in 2 Corinthians 6:17, 'Therefore come out from them and be separate, says the Lord," as meaning that the church should separate itself from the world.

But that stance fails to address Jesus' prayer that we should not be taken from the world. The Scriptures also say we are to be salt and light. It is a paradox: in the world but not of the world.

So, guided by the Spirit of Christ, we must love the world as God does and resist its influence in our lives. Jesus did it. Let us then commit ourselves to follow Him as He leads, wherever He leads.

DAY 62

I n June of the year 2001, a five-year-old boy was mauled to death by his foster mother's Rottweiler in the family's backyard. Kyle Anthony Ross lived with his foster mother, Linda McNeil, who owned the two-year-old male dog. The mom was apparently napping when Kyle approached the dog and was killed. What a horrible, tragic event.

A man who answered the door at the house said, "We ain't got nothing to say, it was an accident."

An animal control officer from the neighboring town of Chicopee removed the dog after the attack. He said the dog has had a history of aggression. "We had a complaint that the dog bit one of the neighbors about a year ago," he said, "but it was nothing of this magnitude."

If you check the news articles over the last several years you will find many stories about people whose dogs maul or kill their neighbors. There is a sick thread that weaves through almost every story: 1) The owners kept dogs that had proven to be dangerous and a threat to the lives and safety of their friends, neighbors and even relatives 2) Even after the dogs had maimed or killed, many of the owners did not want the dogs destroyed.

We tend to treat our "pet" sins the same way. God says that sin will destroy, even kill ("the wages of sin is death" Romans 6:23), and yet we keep them around like these bad dogs—and even when they are exposed, we are often slow to want to get rid of them forever. We often think, like some of these dog owners, that since it is not hurting anyone else, why get rid of it?

But when you became a Christian, you repented of your life of opposition to God, and promised to follow Him. You changed your direction. You responded to God's offer of forgiveness and started a brand-new relationship with Him.

It is a fool's errand to keep a bad dog; it is the same with pet sins. Just because you think you have it on a leash doesn't mean that it cannot get loose and do harm to you and others. You might think that if it is on a long leash, maybe nothing bad will happen. But sooner or later we drift into apathy or sleep and that is when sin attacks. Sin is never your pet, and can never be your friend.

"If you do what is right, will you not be accepted? But if you do not do what is right, sin is crouching at your door; it desires to have you, but you must rule over it." Genesis 4:7

DAY 63

In November of 1992, Kerry Dixon went to the Philippines with a team to work with Christians there. One day, he and his team went to speak to an isolated tribe called the T'boli who lived at Lake Sebu. They took two translators and walked several hours through rough terrain and rice paddies. At about eight in the evening, after nightfall, the word spread that the 'white people' had come. The tribe gathered around the team, lit only by torchlight. Kerry spoke about Jesus through his interpreters to this group that had never heard about Him. After the talk, they pushed forward a middle-aged man, blind from birth, who was well-known and respected in the village. If Jesus was God, they wanted to see Him in action.

In the silence, Kerry laid his hands on the man and prayed for Jesus to heal him. He then asked if the man could see. The man replied through the interpreters that he could see flickering lights through the darkness. After Kerry prayed again, he could make out Kerry's outline in front of him. The third time Kerry prayed—the man began jumping for joy and praising the living God, who had performed a miracle before their eyes. All fifty villagers present that night were converted and a new church begun. That church is still growing today.

Many churches today, especially in third world countries, have been founded by an extraordinary display of God's power. It is amazing to me that in many of those places, one has only to read about Jesus and suddenly people are ready to experience Him. God help us in America if we have become so familiar with the trappings of religion, that we've lost the childlike expectation of seeing God move.

DAY 64

I t still blows me away when I think about the day that I returned. I was so worn out by my own addictions and greed. I was ashamed, tired, exhausted, and filthy—I couldn't stand my own smell. I expected you to send me away, or at the very least, to give me a good lecture and tell me why I could never be your son again. I had run away, had squandered my inheritance, and had wished you dead. Yet, somewhere deep inside, I was secretly hoping for mercy. And while I was still a long way off, silently rehearsing my lines, you spotted me. I saw you lean over the wall trying to get a better look. Suddenly you disappeared. My worst fears were materializing before my weary eyes. But then, I couldn't believe it, I saw you running. At first I thought my eyes were playing a cruel trick on me. You were running to me. Then as you got closer, your robes flying in the wind behind you and the dust kicking up around your feet, I caught your eyes. You ran to me. At first, I couldn't speak. My tears and yours flowed freely. Then I found my voice and I tried to tell you how I had been unfaithful, how I was no longer worthy to be called your son. But you interrupted me. Not with rejection. Not even with the lecture I expected and deserved. But with words of love that shot from your lips like an arrow to my heart. "Welcome home son", you said, "I have been waiting for you". I was crushed, and happy, and so full of emotion I could hardly stand. And then you brought out the best robe, the family ring and the sandals—and the feast. It was a party that beat them all. Father, dad, your love has overwhelmed my shame and made me proud to be your son.

This story, from the perspective of the prodigal son, demonstrates how God feels about those that lose their way. Jesus came to save sinners.

"Here is a trustworthy saying that deserves full acceptance: Christ Jesus came into the world to save sinners—of whom I am the worst." 1 Timothy 1:15. (NIV)

DAY 65

> "Jesus made a whip from some ropes and chased them all out of the Temple. He drove out the sheep and cattle, scattered the money changers' coins over the floor, and turned over their tables." John 2:15 (NLT)

H e sat down and made the whip Himself. This was no flash of rage or impulse. But what was He so angry about?

Jesus, the man of peace, performs a violent act. Everyone seems bewildered. In this age of inclusivity where all are encouraged to "just get along", this act seems almost barbaric.

The priests of the day thought they stood for God. But they had confused respect for themselves and their religious system for true reverence for God. The temple was meant to be a place for people to have access to God; instead, it had become a place of ritual and profit. It became a place where it was hard to find God behind all the rules and expense.

We must be careful not to worship our institutions or programs or buildings. It is a frightening thing for our reverence to only be a reflection of our own glory; where our worship and our life together are all about us and not about God.

Do we reflect today the outlook of the priests of Jesus day rather than that of Jesus Himself? I was once standing near the front of a church building following the morning service, and some children were playing around what was called an 'altar'. A lady came rushing up from somewhere and shouted at the kids "stop playing in here" she yelled, "this is God's house!"

If we say this, we are perpetrating a lie. God doesn't live in buildings. He lives in us. We are His dwelling place!

DAY 66

J esus often said "it is written", and then challenged everyone to obey the teachings in Scripture. Throughout the centuries, those who have done so have found their lives changed.

An atheist once challenged Dr. Harry Ironside to a debate on their beliefs. Dr. Ironside accepted the challenge but proposed that his rival bring with him to the hall two people—one man who was for years under the power of evil habits from which he could not deliver himself, but who had heard the glorification of atheism, and had his life revolutionized for the better. Ironside also asked the atheist to bring a woman who was similarly delivered from corrupt living by the power of unbelief.

Dr. Ironside then offered to bring one-hundred men and women who for years lived in a similar state, but had been gloriously saved and changed through believing the gospel. The atheist walked away confessing his inability to produce even one person.

So how do we convince others of the truth of our position? There is no need to. While we should always be prepared to explain why we believe the Bible to be the Word of God, there is little point of trying to convince others. They must find out for themselves.

Charles Spurgeon said defending the Bible is like defending a caged lion. It is foolish to stand outside the cage with a sword to protect the lion from its enemies. The most effective way to defend the lion is to open the cage and let it go. The Bible, just like the lion, is perfectly capable of looking after itself. The best way to convince people that it is the Word of God is to have them read it for themselves and put into practice what it says.

DAY 67

"Jesus replied, "The most important commandment is this: 'You must love the Lord your God with all your heart, all your soul, all your mind, and all your strength.' The second is equally important: 'Love your neighbor as yourself.' No other commandment is greater than these." Mark 12:29-31

For Jewish religious associations, like the Qumran communities, the Essenes, and the Pharisees--life centered around a CODE (or a set of rules), as embodied in the Torah. This lay at the basis of blessings, readings, expositions, confessions, and prayers that formed the content of the synagogue services.

For members of the Hellenistic Jews, life centered primarily around a cult, with dramatic rituals, processions, and mystical experiences.

The Scriptures teach that the Christian Life centers primarily around FELLOWSHIP with God and one another. The gifts and fruit of the Spirit are the instruments through which this fellowship is expressed and deepened.

This means that the focal point for Christians is not a book or a rite, not a code or a cult, but a set of relationships: love God, love neighbor.

It seems to me that Catholicism increasingly followed the path of the cults in making a rite the center of its activities as Protestantism followed the path of the synagogue in placing a book and rules at the center of its services. Of course, the Bible and communion and moral rules are fundamental to what takes place in church, but there is more to the work of the Spirit in the church than the Word and Sacrament and good behavior. To separate the Word and Sacrament from the relationship is to indulge in empty religious exercise; to separate moral behavior from the relationship is to become a legalist. All of these are empty without God.

DAY 68

> "Jesus replied, "'You must love the Lord your God with all your heart, all your soul, and all your mind.' This is the first and greatest commandment. A second is equally important: 'Love your neighbor as yourself.' The entire law and all the demands of the prophets are based on these two commandments." Matthew 22:37-40 (NLT)

J esus had just been asked by a lawyer what the most important commandment was in the Law of Moses. Jesus, sounding more like a hippy than a preacher, replied "It's all about love."

Then He went a step further and mentioned the second most important command: love your neighbor.

Love, love, love. What in the world was Jesus trying to say?

We should remember that Jesus is talking to a group of people who have spent much of their time defining the legal specifics of God's law. They had become so consumed by law keeping, that they had made up rules around the law so they couldn't possibly be accused of breaking Moses' law. These rules were called traditions.

In Matthew 15, Jesus tells the religious leaders of Israel that they were using their traditions to violate the direct commandments of God. They were so tied to the letter of the law that they violated its' spirit. They were rule keepers, but not lovers. It is easier to keep rules than it is to love someone.

Jesus' correction of their error was to talk about relationship. Love God with everything that you are: heart, soul and mind. And love your neighbor as you love yourself.

If you truly love God with all your heart you will naturally desire to please Him in everything you do. And if you love your neighbor as yourself, you will treat them with the same care and respect you wish to receive. When these two loves are lived out, they fulfill the entire message of Scripture.

127

But we can't do this in our own strength. We need the Holy Spirit living within us—and that begins with surrendering our lives to Jesus. It all flows from relationship with Him then out to those around us. Even our enemies.

The demands of the gospel sometimes seem so outrageous, and that is why it is easy for me to believe it could not be a construction from the human mind.

DAY 69

Jesus says, in John 13:34, "So now I am giving you a new commandment: Love each other. Just as I have loved you, you should love each other."

L iving in community with other believers is difficult to do. The idea that the church is a building or even just a meeting is foreign to the New Testament. The church is the people of God gathered, and we are called to live in relationship with each other; we are called to love each other. But the world pressures us to devote ourselves to gain a sense of personal security and significance before we get around to obeying God and loving others.

Yet, we should be ready for confusion and disappointment. Why? Because that's part of following Christ into community. There are no pat and easy answers. How do we love the sinner but hate the sin—how do we reject the sin without rejecting the sinner? How do we die to ourselves? Why is so much of life disappointing? Why don't people behave and why do bad things happen to good people?

Those questions throw us into dependence upon the Holy Spirit. Spiritual community is only possible by the presence and power of the Spirit. If we don't see the power of God manifested in our lives, we won't have the faith to believe that He can and will change us. There are many in America whose hunger for piety is great, but they live in constant frustration because they don't know if God can really change their lives. They haven't seen signs of God's power and presence. If we want to have faith for changed lives and power to love others, we need to continually live in Jesus and have His life poured into ours.

DAY 70

Jesus seemed to be able to touch others because He did not recoil from their pain—He did not try to always explain it, or fix it; He sometimes just lived it with them.

When Lazarus had died, his sister Mary came out to meet Jesus. When He saw her weeping, and the Jews who had come along with her also weeping, He was deeply moved in spirit and troubled. "Where have you laid him?" He asked. "Come and see, Lord," they replied. Jesus wept.

Pain must be shared in order to be comforted and healed. Jesus did not rise above all the pain in the world like some stoic Greek god— He choose instead to participate in our suffering. He literally became one of us: The Word became flesh and dwelt among us, John writes. Jesus shared our humanity—He lived in our skin. He laughed and cried with us so that we can be caught up into His joy and be comforted by His gentle care.

Surely by the time Jesus arrived, He knew He was going to raise Lazarus from the dead. If this scene were made in Hollywood, Jesus might have waltzed into town saying "no worries, I've got this"— showing off His power at the expense of other's grief.

But instead, He comes and shares in the suffering of the world that was caused when Satan's lies and humanity's rebellion kissed. Jesus embraces the loss and pain of death even as He comes to conquer it. He takes Mary's rebuff — "Lord, if you had been here, my brother would not have died." And responds in tears.

Jesus is never far from us; even in our pain and sadness, He is always there ready to embrace us and share our troubles.

"All praise to God, the Father of our Lord Jesus Christ. God is our merciful Father and the source of all comfort. He comforts us in all our troubles so that we can comfort others. When they are troubled, we will be able to give them the same comfort God has given us." 2 Corinthians 1: 3-4 (NLT)

DAY 71

"Jesus went into Galilee, proclaiming the good news of God. 'The time has come,' He said. 'The Kingdom of God has come near. Repent and believe the good news!'" Mark 1:14-15 (NIV)

What is the best government in the world? Is it capitalism, communism, Kings and Queens, or some variance of any or all of them? It is hard for us to imagine a perfect system. We know we are broken, and we see some of the most dysfunctional brokenness in our governments. Can broken people develop a nearly-perfect system of governance? It really doesn't seem so.

Where is God in all this? Where is this good news? God invaded this world in Jesus Christ to establish the foothold of His Kingdom on this earth. But that was just the start. The will of God is still allowed to be thwarted by human will and the devil.

So, what does Jesus mean when He talks about the Kingdom of God? If the Kingdom of God has come, why is there still so much nastiness and brokenness in the world? Why are there still so many wars and riots and deaths and diseases?

It's because the Kingdom of God has invaded this world through Jesus, but it won't be consummated until He returns. We experience the Kingdom partially now, but will not experience it fully until Jesus returns to earth. And He is waiting, waiting for the fullness of time when everyone has had the opportunity to hear the good news according to Matthew 24:14, "And this gospel of the Kingdom will be proclaimed throughout the whole world as a testimony to all nations, and then the end will come."

But for now, when we see salvation, deliverance or healing and wholeness in Jesus' name, that is the presence of the Kingdom. One day God will end all violence and heal all brokenness, but that is in the future. Today, we only experience the Kingdom of God partially. We must pray "Jesus, let Your Kingdom come, Your will be done on earth as it is in Heaven." Then we look for His Kingdom to manifest in our lives and in our communities as we follow Him and do His bidding.

The Kingdom of God is consummated when Jesus is truly King over all of creation—when He returns creation will run on one simple thing: our world will run on the will of God. And neither the will of mankind nor the will of Satan will thwart it.

DAY 72

J ust after midnight on Christmas morning, the majority of German troops engaged in World War I cease firing their guns and artillery, and commence to sing Christmas carols. At certain points along the Eastern and Western fronts, the soldiers of Russia, France, and Britain even hear brass bands joining the Germans in their joyous singing. At the first light of dawn, many of the German soldiers emerge from their trenches and approach the Allied lines across no man's land, calling out "Merry Christmas" in their enemies' native tongues.

At first the Allied soldiers suspect it to be a trick, but they too soon climb out of their trenches and shake hands with the German soldiers. The men exchange presents of cigarettes and plum puddings and sing carols and songs and the Christmas Truce lasts a few days. There is even a documented case of soldiers from opposing sides playing a good-natured game of football, also known as soccer. The Christmas Truce of 1914 comes only five months after the outbreak of war in Europe, and is one of the last examples of the outdated notion of chivalry in warfare. Over the next year, the bloody conflict of World War I erupts in all its technological fury, and the idea of another Christmas Truce becomes unthinkable.

This story fascinated me because no one was killed, there was goodwill in the midst of war, and the truce lasted for several days. What a miracle!

It is a story that conveys the truth that light can spring out of darkness, if even for a brief season, because of the gift of God's Son, Jesus. May your Christmas—in whatever circumstances you find yourself—have at least a truce of hope and peace that overflows into goodwill to others.

DAY 73

"Keep your lives free from the love of money and be content with what you have, because God has said, 'Never will I leave you; never will I forsake you.' So we say with confidence, 'The Lord is my helper; I will not be afraid. What can man do to me?'" Hebrews 13:5-6 (NIV)

W e worry because we are afraid. Afraid we won't have enough; afraid that what we have is not adequate. We fear because we don't know what might happen next; just like we fear the dark room, not because there is something in there, but because we don't know what *might* be there.

Biologists believe that fear is among the first and strongest emotions developed in man and animal. Fear and anxiety haunt us and can absolutely paralyze us. We fear what happens outside our control. God wants us to trust Him.

The only answer to this fear is Jesus; the one who will never leave us alone. When John saw the risen Christ in His glory on the isle of Patmos, he said, "When I saw Him, I fell at His feet as dead. But He laid His right hand on me and said, 'Don't be afraid! I am the First and the Last. I am the living one who died. Look, I am alive forever and ever! And I hold the keys of death and the grave.'" Revelation 1:17-18 (NLT)

When the angel brought his message to Mary, he said, "Don't fear." When Jesus called Peter to follow Him, He said, "Simon, don't be afraid!" When speaking to Jairus about his daughter in Luke 8, Jesus said, "Don't be afraid, just trust me."

It was the manifest presence of Jesus that calmed the disciples' fears. *Christ never says to us, "Don't fear, here is a million dollars," or "Don't fear, here is a miraculous drug." He says, "Don't fear. It's me. Trust me." Jesus' presence always drove out fear and it still does. Our greatest strength during times of fear is the manifest presence of Jesus.*

DAY 74

"No one sews a patch of unshrunk cloth on an old garment. Otherwise, the new piece will pull away from the old, making the tear worse. And no one pours new wine into old wineskins. Otherwise, the wine will burst the skins, and both the wine and the wineskins will be ruined. No, they pour new wine into new wineskins." Mark 2: 21-22 (NIV)

King Hezekiah of Judah went on a mission from God. The second book of Kings records Hezekiah's reforms—going around and demolishing things and places that were used for idol worship. One of the things he destroyed was the bronze snake that Moses had made.

If you remember the story, the Israelites had sinned and God had punished them with venomous snakes. After many people had died, the nation repented of their sin and God instructed Moses to build a bronze snake so that everyone who looked on it would live, even if they had been bitten.

There are churches today where people have been using the same method for years and years. That method may have been successful in the past, but there is a limited life cycle on any method. Church members often defend old methods by saying, "This is the way we have always done it." Do you realize, for instance, that it is not recorded that Paul ever gave an invitation for people to come forward in a service for salvation? That kind of invitation was an invention of the evangelist Dwight L. Moody. That is only one method that God has given us. God led Moody to do it, with great success, but that doesn't mean everyone should do it.

We are often tempted to hang on to past successes even when God has already moved on. The brazen serpent was once by God to deliver Israel from judgment, but after that it was just snake on a stick. Sometimes God uses methods and means that at one time serve a purpose and are mightily used by Him, but then their usefulness comes to an end. Anything God has successfully used in the past can become a present-day idol.

DAY 75

"My brothers and sisters, God called you to be free, but do not use
your freedom as an excuse to do what pleases your sinful self.
Serve each other with love." Galatians 5:13 (NCV)

In Galatians 5:13, Paul reminds Christians that freedom in Christ does not mean doing whatever we want to please ourselves. True freedom is not about self-indulgence; it's about serving others with love. Paul emphasizes that we are free from sin, but we are also bound by the "law of love," which means we are called to love God and others above all else.

Freedom without boundaries leads to chaos, and that's why Paul contrasts being "free from sin" with being "slaves to righteousness." This doesn't mean that we're perfect or without sin. Instead, it means we are no longer controlled by sin. Through Christ, we now have the ability to choose righteousness. Before salvation, sin was our master, but now, in Christ, we are free from its power and are called to serve God.

Some believe that freedom in Christ means automatic righteousness, but the New Testament teaches that we can still choose to sin. In 1 John chapter one, it says if we claim to be without sin, we deceive ourselves. But God has given us provision: He is faithful to forgive and cleanse us when we confess.

Ultimately, true freedom in Christ means choosing to live in a way that honors God and helps others. Our freedom is not for self-indulgence but to serve others in love, avoiding actions that may lead others astray. Loving God and loving our neighbors are the greatest commandments, and as Christians, we are called to live by them, serving both God and others with joy and humility.

DAY 76

> "Make sure that no one is immoral or godless like Esau, who traded his birthright as the firstborn son for a single meal. You know that afterward, when he wanted his father's blessing, he was rejected. It was too late for repentance, even though he begged with bitter tears." Hebrews 12:16-17 (NLT)

J esus began His ministry by preaching repentance, and the church began the same way. When God finally steps on the stage and closes the book on history, we see that the condemned resist God to the very end. Christianity is all about not resisting God; it is birthed and cradled in repentance.

Some believe that you just need to repent to get in and then you're done with it. To repent means to quit my resistance to the Holy Spirit, see matters God's way, turn from my way, and follow Him.

As with Esau, God's Spirit strives patiently with those who resist Him, but will eventually let such people have their own way. His Spirit will not always strive with us. Esau had sinned in selling his birthright, and clearly went on resisting the Holy Spirit for years. Finally, he was unable to repent even though he tried to with tears.

I don't know of any Scripture that tells me to take my sin to God and ask Him to deliver me from it and then trust in faith that He will. God promises to deliver us from the power of sin—that is, to make sin no longer irresistible. But it is up to us to repent—to keep our accounts with God short, and to resist sin. We must repent and believe...and keep on repenting and believing. Daily. If you don't, a time may come, like with Esau, when you are unable to repent even though you plead with bitter tears.

DAY 77

J ust as there are any people today that are convinced that the devil is not real, there are also those who seemed obsessed with the devil and his dark kingdom.

C. S. Lewis nailed it when he wrote, "There are two equal and opposite errors into which our race can fall about the devils. One is to disbelieve in their existence. The other is to believe, and to feel an excessive and unhealthy interest in them."

But the reason you should believe devils are real is because the Bible treats them as such. The kingdom of darkness led by the dark lord is at war with the Kingdom of God. The book of Revelation says this of the antichrist: "he was given power to make war against the saints and to conquer them. And he was given authority over every tribe, people, language and nation" (Chapter 13). It behooves us to know about such a formidable foe, to neither fear him nor to dismiss him.

In his remarkable book, *Hostage to the Devil*, Martin Malachi tells the story of five contemporary Americans who were possessed by devils. Here is one account shared from that book in which an Exorcist by the name of Gerald attempted to free a person from the grip possession:

"Gerald straightened up. He changed his tone to a sharp, inquisitorial, and imperious note: 'You, evil spirit, you will obey our commands.' Again, the rasping voice: 'You do not know what you're getting into, priest. You cannot pay the price. It's not your virginity merely that you'll lose. And not merely your life. You'll lose it all—' 'As Jesus, Our Lord, bore sufferings, so I am willing to bear what it costs to expel you and send you back to where you came from.'"

This was Gerald's first error. Without realizing it, and in what looked like heroism, he had fallen into an old trap. They were now on a personal plane: he versus the evil spirit. No exorcist can function in a personal way, in his own right, offering his strength or his will alone to counter and challenge the possessing spirit. He never should try to function in place of

Jesus, but merely speak and act in concert with Him as His representative. For Gerald the cost of that mistake was high. He had never dreamed that physical punishment could be so intense. It was a full three weeks before he could get up and hobble around his room in great pain; that violent attack on him would eventually prove lethal for Gerald."

Even those whose work is to directly confront the enemy are not immune to their wiles or strengths. We would do well to learn from these works— not to induce fear, but to engage in good strategies given by the Holy Spirit in order to defeat the enemy.

DAY 78

S ometimes people sit around waiting for the church to do the work of ministry. But in the New Testament, the church is not a building or a meeting; the church is literally 'the called-out ones'; it is the people of God.

A young man once approached his pastor on a Sunday morning, upset because he felt like the church wasn't doing its job. On the previous Monday, he had met a man while going to work. This man was out of work and homeless, and had nothing to eat for a while. "I felt sorry for him" the young man said, "so I told him I would try to help him out. I called the church and no one answered, so I went out and got this guy some food, and told him he could stay at my house that night until we could get him some help. The next day, I called the church and still couldn't get anyone, so I had to help this guy find a job. I've spent my whole week trying to get this guy some help and I just want to know when the church is going to start doing its job and get this guy some help."

"Well," the pastor replied, "it sounds like the church did its job."

The church is not a building or an organization; it is a community of people who are committed to serving God and His cause.

If you are a believer, you are a part of the church and you have a ministry. In fact, ministry can be defined as meeting people's needs with God's resources. You are part of God's resources; in God's hands, you become the carrier of the life of Christ to a world in need. And if you've been a believer for a while, God is ready for you to take those training wheels off your bike!

"No prolonged infancies among us, please. We'll not tolerate babes in the woods, small children who are easy prey for predators. God wants us to grow up, to know the whole truth and tell it in love—like Christ in everything. We take our lead from Christ, who is the source of everything we do. He keeps us in step with each other. His very breath and blood flow through us, nourishing us so that we will grow up healthy in God, robust in love." Ephesians 4: 14-16 (The Message)

DAY 79

Matthew 5:3(NLT) says, "God blesses those who are poor and realize their need for Him, for the Kingdom of Heaven is theirs."

B lessed are the underprivileged, the downcast, and the have-nots. Blessed are the marginalized—those who know they are spiritually bankrupt. There is no particular virtue in poverty; but there is virtue in knowing your poverty.

Of course, the world has a different standard. The world's standard is blessed are the beautiful, the powerful, and the privileged; those who are easily noticed, unique, and not hard to look at. No one wants to recognize their poverty because poverty equals weakness and no one in their right mind wants to be seen as weak.

In church we often give voice to the worlds' standard. You may have heard the phrase, sometimes given as an invitation at the end of a service, for people to 'make a decision for Christ'. But is that really what God wants? He asks us to follow Him and to yield to Him, but those things don't rely on our strength, but on our weakness. To yield means to recognize our own poverty. That means we cannot enter into His Kingdom because of our goodness, or our standing, or our resources; we can only enter the Kingdom as have-nots.

In other words, we must recognize that we are a needy and broken people. We don't need a guru to give us words to live by. We need a savior to save us from our sin and depravity. We are powerless to save ourselves. It is in our poverty that God meets us; when there is less of us, there is more of Him. Our poverty makes room for God in our lives, and in our poverty, we are truly blessed.

DAY 80

"In the morning, O Lord, You will hear my voice; In the morning I will prepare [a prayer and a sacrifice] for You and watch and wait [for You to speak to my heart]." Psalm 5:3 (Amplified Bible)

Morning prayer has been a cornerstone of spiritual life across various cultures and religions throughout history, serving as a time for reflection, gratitude, and supplication. An example of the significance of morning prayer can be found in the story of the Pilgrims' arrival in the New World. In December 1620, the Pilgrims aboard the Mayflower faced severe hardships upon reaching what is now Plymouth, Massachusetts. Their journey had been fraught with peril, and their arrival marked the beginning of a struggle for survival in an unforgiving land.

The Pilgrims were a group of English Separatists seeking religious freedom from the Church of England. Their voyage was driven by a desire to practice their faith without persecution. Upon landing, they faced harsh winter conditions, inadequate supplies, and an uncertain future. Despite these challenges, the Pilgrims' commitment to prayer remained steadfast.

The morning of December 11, 1620, marked a significant moment in their ordeal. The Pilgrims held a solemn morning prayer service, which was not just a ritual but a vital source of strength and resolve. This morning service was a beacon of hope, providing the settlers with the fortitude needed to face their difficult and sometimes deadly circumstances.

Their morning prayers were the foundation of their broader spiritual resilience. It was not merely an act of devotion but a fundamental component of their daily lives, grounding them in faith in God and his purpose for their lives. The act of coming together in prayer each morning reinforced their sense of unity and purpose, helping them navigate the uncertainties of their new environment together.

Morning prayer can serve as a powerful tool for perseverance and communal strength in the face of adversity. The Pilgrims' experience illustrates that morning prayer provided them with the emotional and spiritual fortitude required to overcome the numerous challenges they faced.

I know that some of you, like me, are not "morning persons". But I must say that after all this time as a believer, beginning my day with prayer, knowing that others are at the same time talking to God, gives my day a certain resolve and resilience and helps prepare me for whatever circumstances may bring.

DAY 81

"In repentance and rest is your salvation, in quietness and trust is your strength." Isaiah 30:15 (NIV)

M ost Christians are not deeply rooted in a life of unhurried peace and rest. Many live hurried, distracted, and anxious lives—rushing from one commitment to the next, often feeling spiritually tired even while doing "good things."

Many families still struggle with decisions about money, possessions, and time. Priorities based on values are rarely discussed. We are so overwhelmed by consumerism through advertising and the 'desire for more' that we seldom realize it is the air we breathe every day. Our uncontrollable desires drive us more than we want to admit. Money disagreements and priorities are the top reasons for divorce in America.

But our culture is not only plagued by the passion to possess, it is plagued by its busyness. Not only do we rush to accumulate more, but we and our children rush to achieve more—to experience more. We are driven by a compulsion to experience more and more of life. The rat race has never been more frantic and driven. We race through an endless series of appointments and duties; of family and business obligations. Jackson Browne expressed this social malaise well in his song *Running on Empty*. He said, "Looking into their eyes, I see they're running too."

Christian Simplicity frees us from the modern mania of compulsive extravagance and gives an unhurried peace to our frantic spirit. It allows us to see material things as goods to enhance life; not to oppress it. Christian Simplicity makes people more important than things. It also helps us develop a strategy for addressing social inequities, wasted lives, and meaningless activities.

This witness to Simplicity is firmly rooted in the biblical tradition as is perfectly exemplified in the life of Jesus Christ. Don't confuse Simplicity with being simplistic. The journey into Simplicity is complex. It will demand a rearranging of your priorities–doing the most important things first.

DAY 82

M any Christians assume their hunger for God's presence ranks very high on their list—often far higher than it really does. Many are blind to the half-hearted obeisance they offer God on a daily basis. Their flame of passion has died down to a lit matchstick. How passionate are you for God? If you approach this question in all honesty, asking God to help you see the truth, what would your response be?

We declare that we want to see transforming revival, but first we need to determine our readiness for it. We begin by asking God to cleanse our hearts and to rid us of our idolatries. A. W. Pink says: "A 'god' whose will is resisted, whose designs are frustrated, whose purpose is checkmated, possesses no title to Deity, and so far from being a fit object of worship, merits naught but contempt." Our lives and daily habits reflect our contempt for God. Many of us have been giving lip service to a god of our own invention; a god that is too small. We need to repent of not seeing God as He is: worthy of our worship, worthy of our best, worthy of our all. Does not the Bible say in Luke 10, "Love the Lord your God with ALL your heart and with ALL your soul and with ALL your strength and with ALL your mind?" Luke 10:27 (NIV) Love God with absolute abandon.

Along with the Psalmist we need to cry out:

> "Search me, O God, and know my heart; test me and know my anxious thoughts. See if there is any offensive way in me, and lead me in the way everlasting." Psalm 139:23-24 (NIV)

So why is it important to evaluate ourselves this way? *Because transforming revival is triggered the moment our appetite for God's presence trumps all other hungers in our lives.* We become like the person who found a treasure in a field and sold everything to get it:

> "The Kingdom of Heaven is like treasure hidden in a field. When a man found it, he hid it again, and then in his joy went and sold all he had and bought that field." Matthew 13:44 (NIV)

Do you remember your first real encounter with the Lord Jesus? I couldn't stop smiling, I couldn't stop telling everyone, He was such good news to me! Are you in darkness? He is the light. Are you feeling alone and outside? He is the door. Are you hungry and thirsty? He is the living water and the bread of life. As He becomes our sustenance, our very provision and passion for life, we will see and experience a genuine revival!

DAY 83

"My barn having burned to the ground; I can now see the moon."
— Masahide

After suffering two heart attacks, by-pass surgery, Atrial Fibrillation, and then in a 2012 diagnosis of congestive heart failure, my doctors suggested a heart transplant. My wife and I prayed and talked. We also shared it with our children since we had a rule that everyone in the family had a voice in every major decision we made. I could not believe I needed a heart transplant. I knew I had a new normal—I could only shuffle five or six feet without becoming winded—but a heart transplant? I had never known anybody that had undergone that surgery. I was old enough to remember the first heart transplant that happened one year after my high school graduation. I didn't remember the patient but I did remember the doctor— surgeon Christian Barnard from South Africa, and that the patient had lived less than three weeks! So, I had the transplant.

In looking back, I am first of all extremely grateful—this seems so much like a second chance. But I have also learned something about faith. As we prayed expectantly for my healing, and lived within this tension of faith and the lack of certainty, I became more and more convinced that God simply wanted me to trust him no matter the outcome. I learned that faith is not faith if you are holding the answer. Faith is out there swinging in the breeze, just beyond our sight, but it is a reality nevertheless as substantial as the ground we walk on. As the Japanese poet Masahide wrote, "My barn having burned to the ground; I can now see the moon". I believe he meant that when something difficult occurs, something else becomes possible. For me, I saw not only the moon more clearly, but beheld more clearly and brightly the light of Christ.

Paul writes to the church,

"We can rejoice, too, when we run into problems and trials, for we know that they help us develop endurance." Romans 5:3 (NLT)

So, as my life seemingly burned to the ground, I saw endurance rising in my heart from the ashes of my former life. Some things must leave before we can see what treasure might have been hidden from us.

"Listen carefully: Unless a grain of wheat is buried in the ground, dead to the world, it is never any more than a grain of wheat. But if it is buried, it sprouts and reproduces itself many times over. In the same way, anyone who holds on to life just as it is destroys that life. But if you let it go, reckless in your love, you'll have it forever, real and eternal." John 12: 24-25 (The Message)

DAY 84

"My ears had heard of You before, but now my eyes have seen You." Job 42:5 (NCV)

G od said Job was a good man. But in response to Satan's condemnation, God allowed Satan to inflict whatever pain he wished—short of taking Job's life. Job lost his fortune, his children and his health.

In terrible anguish and profound depression, Job refused to despair or curse God and die (even though his wife encouraged him to do just that). His friends accused him of sin. God is not to blame, they said, so the blame must be Job's. And Job had some questions for God, and believed that if he could just talk to God, He would confirm that Job had done nothing wrong.

Then God shows up, but apparently not just to talk. God shows up in a whirlwind; perhaps a little terrifying and awe-inspiring.

And now God has questions. Where was Job when God created the earth or the seas or the heavens? God is not showing off, or being haughty. God's correction is designed to restore and improve Job's viewpoint. It's clear that God still cares for Job. But Job is not vindicated by his own goodness but by God's mercy, even as his own friends stand corrected.

The fact that Job ends up with twice as much as he lost may not mean much. We are suspicious of "happily ever after" stories. Yet in Job's era, things like children and prosperity were signs of God's approval. Pain is not necessarily judgment. Those that God loves may endure troubles that are unrelated to sin or divine wrath.

Something greater than prosperity had invaded Job's life; a richness brought by experiencing and treasuring the majesty and glory of God. "Now my eyes have seen you." If we begin to catch even a glimpse of God's awesomeness, we may feel like we are on our toes peeking over Job's shoulder. And what a sight it is.

DAY 85

Mythic stories like those of Hernan Cortes' taking of Veracruz in 1519 and Tariq ibn Ziyad taking of Gibraltar in 711, telling their men to burn their ships thereby cutting off all chances of retreat, have been used to motivate people for many years. The stories follow the same pattern: They had landed on enemy land in order to conquer them, then they either burned or scuttled their ships so there could only be victory or death. They both succeeded in their mission. These stories usually end with a motivational statement like, "to truly achieve the level of success we desire, there are times we need to 'burn our ships'", i.e., we need to cut off our little escape routes so that we do or die. It motivates us to succeed. So, identify your ships that need burning and move on to success!

Jesus used a different approach to commitment, and it kept the freedom of will in place: "When you plow, don't look back"; to the disciples He said, "would you abandon me now?" but they replied "where else would we go?" "Unless you hate your mother and father," Jesus said, "you cannot be my disciple." Further, He says, "to gain you must lose; a seed must die to grow, and you must die to really live."

In the end, Jesus is not just some motivational speaker. He is God and He challenges us to live as if we were totally committed to Him, His cause, and His mission in the world. Then He goes on to demonstrate what that looks like.

He's holding up a mirror. What do you see when you look at your life? Does it reflect the belief that Jesus is God and His demands are not just worth following, but are the only way? Jesus is the way, the truth and life. He's not a way. He's not a truth. He's not a life. He Himself is abundant life.

"Jesus said to him, "I am the way, the truth, and the life. No one comes to the Father except through me." John 14:6 (NKJV)

DAY 86

Newspaper columnist and minister George Crane tells of a wife who came into his office full of hatred toward her husband. "I do not only want to get rid of him, I want to get even. Before I divorce him, I want to hurt him as much as he has me."

Dr. Crane suggested an ingenious plan "Go home and act as if you really love your husband. Tell him how much he means to you. Praise him for every decent trait. Go out of your way to be as kind, considerate, and generous as possible. Spare no efforts to please him, to enjoy him. Make him believe you love him. After you've convinced him of your undying love and that you cannot live without him, then drop the bomb. Tell him that you're getting a divorce. That will really hurt him."

With revenge in her eyes, she smiled and exclaimed, "Beautiful, beautiful. Will he ever be surprised!" And she did it with enthusiasm; acting "as if she really loved him." For two months she showed love, kindness, listening, giving, reinforcing, and sharing.

When she didn't return, Crane called. "Are you ready now to go through with the divorce?" "Divorce?" she exclaimed. "Never! I discovered I really do love him."

Her actions had changed her feelings. Motion had resulted in emotion. The ability to love is established not so much by enthusiastic promises but the habit of repeated deeds.

Being in love is a good thing, but it is not the best thing. Love is a deep unity kept willfully and deliberately. It is strengthened by habits and reinforced by God's grace. In the words of C. S. Lewis: This is the kind of love that fuels marriage; being in love was simply the explosion that started it.

DAY 87

"No discipline seems pleasant at the time, but painful. Later on, however, it produces a harvest of righteousness and peace for those who have been trained by it. Therefore, strengthen your feeble arms and weak knees. 'Make level paths for your feet,' so that the lame may not be disabled, but rather healed." Hebrews 12:11-13 (NIV)

I t has been said that the church is the only institution that shoots its wounded. When there has been moral failure or exposed sin, or even just questionable behavior, then the church has been quick to punish. Excommunication, while not formally practiced, has been informally exercised in the church. People who don't measure up are often ostracized or put down or maligned. The truth is, sheep bite.

But the Scriptures call us to accountability. Some sins require public action. But there is never a call to punish. There is no call to condemn. Still there is much confusion. Some say, "we are not to judge" referring to Jesus' words in Matthew seven, yet Paul says in I Corinthians 5:12 that we are to judge those inside the church who are sinning.

In the passage in Matthew seven Jesus tells us to judge ourselves first, before judging others. In First Corinthians, Paul is telling us to be responsible and hold those who continue to practice willful sin accountable.

But what about those who are not willfully continuing in sin, but have fallen? How do we treat them? Even Christians sometimes morbidly love a good hanging. We sometimes secretly delight in the fall of another. We want to see the guilty punished.

Church discipline should look more like setting a broken bone than just breaking bones. We should be careful, Paul warns the Galatians, when we help someone in sin that we don't fall into the same temptation ourselves.

We need less indignation and more gentleness and humility. Sin has its own wages—it pays only death. We are never the "Christian Mafia." Our job is not to break bones, but heal them.

DAY 88

"No one whose hope is in You will ever be put to shame." Psalms 25:3 (NIV)

G uilt comes from doing wrong things; shame comes from a sense that something's wrong with us. Guilt says, "I have done something wrong." Shame says, "There is something wrong with me."

We deal with our shame by creating a facade. It is an image that we project to everyone around us. It is a lie. We want people to believe that we are better than we are. In Greek plays, the actors who wore masks were called hypocrites—literally two-faced. That is where we get our word hypocrisy.

In the Garden of Eden Adam and Eve were both naked yet they were without shame. But once they rebelled against God, they became shameful and hid from Him. That has been the lot of all humanity since; we feel shamed and hide from God.

But God never intended for us to live like that. Jesus took our shame and guilt to the cross. The book of Hebrews says that Jesus endured the cross, and scorned its shame: the shame of an innocent man being hung on a cross as a common criminal.

He died so we can follow Him into death; He rose from the dead to give us real life. That life is intended to be free from shame. God, through Christ, offers us the chance to get rid of our false selves—to be at peace with ourselves because God has fully embraced us, embracing us even in our shame and our brokenness. He has loved us so deeply that, if we will let Him, His love will drive out all our guilt and shame. And we will find ourselves running to Him rather than from Him.

DAY 89

"Now faith is the substance of things hoped for, the evidence of things not seen. For by it the elders obtained a good testimony. By faith we understand that the worlds were framed by the word of God, so that the things which are seen were not made of things which are visible." Hebrews 11:1-3 (NKJV)

"So faith comes from hearing, and hearing by the word of Christ." Romans 10:17 (NASB)

I t does not say, "faith comes from seeing, and seeing by your assumptions."

In the fall of 2002, a sniper in the DC area shot people at a gas station, leaving Home Depot, and walking down the street. These attacks went on in a variety of places for over three weeks and resulted in the deaths of ten people. During this time, as you can imagine, people were terrified to leave their homes, go shopping, or even walk through their neighborhoods. Police officers and the FBI worked frantically to solve the crimes, and a tip hotline was set up. Law enforcement received over 140,000 tips, which resulted in approximately 35,000 possible suspects.

Most of the tips were dead ends, until a white van was spotted at the site of one of the shootings. The police chief went on national television with a picture of the white van. After the news conference, several other eyewitnesses called to say that they too had seen a white van fleeing from the scene of the shooting. At the time, there were more than 70,000 white vans in the area. Police officers, as well as the general public, focused almost exclusively on white vans because they believed the eyewitnesses. Other tips were ignored. When the suspects were finally caught, they were driving a blue sedan.

Suggestibility and preconceptions are huge factors in determining truth. Some people say that they would believe if only they could see a "miracle," not understanding that if they are prejudiced against miracles, then they are more likely to explain away any miracle even if they saw it with their own eyes. Faith comes by hearing...and hearing by the Word of God. In other words, for us to exercise faith, we must be influenced by the Word—you believe to see; you do not need to see to believe.

DAY 90

O ne of the things in our society that people do not wish to talk about is death. Here in America, we sanitize our dead. We get them to the morgue as quickly as possible, have the bodies prepared for burial and disguised to look "normal."

That is not true in every place in the world. In some of the third- world countries I have visited, death looks very different. Sometimes the bodies of the dead are taken by women into the home, put on the table, washed, dressed, and prepared for burial. Then there is a wake for people to come by to pay their respects. The body is not snatched away, time is given to prepare for the loss.

I was happy to hear, only recently, that many hospitals are now allowing a different process for the death of infants. They have a special "cooling bed" that, after cleaning the body of the baby, allows mothers to come in and sit with them as long as they like. The cooling bed prevents rapid decay. This allows death to be processed in a healthy way.

But we don't really want our lives to be bothered by death. Death is no longer our constant companion. Until the twentieth century most children died before they were ten, and adults died at home with the family around them.

María Antonieta Sánchez de Escamilla, a Kindergarten teacher in Mexico, wrote: "I tell my pupils to live each day as if it were their last... I don't want children to fear death; I want them to respect life... It's good for children to confront the idea of death, and... of their own mortality. Sometimes a child feels squeamish about death... skulls and skeletons. When this happens, I tell my pupils to touch themselves. 'Why are you afraid?' I ask, 'when each of you owns a skull and skeleton. We all carry death within us.' They feel themselves, and they say: 'Yes it's true, we too are made of bones.'"

It has become normal to think as if we are all going to live in this world forever. Death, once embraced as a normal part of life, is now a reason to doubt the goodness of God.

If we understand the biblical worldview, then death loses its sting. In the past, Christians saw this life as a preparation for the next. There was much literature written on dying well. It is true that we are literally born dying. Our inability to face death head-on in this generation has caused great anxiety and fear to grow. I heard this story not long ago about a man named Reed Grafke. What he says, as he is nearing death, is a wonderful tribute to a life lived for God.

"Things are winding down for me and my life's message is oozing out in small ways to this present as I go. One thing I have never imagined about walking through this last thin place is that when you have been yielded to God for years, it is not a giant step into eternity. Rather, it is just another small step over an ever-thinning line. I can see the line from here and am just living each moment as I take the next few steps. As I approach the line, I don't have to get a running start or jump over any hurdles. It will just be the next little step. I think I am ready and I'm happy to share with you as your time and my energy permits."

DAY 91

O ur sins are not just "bad habits." Christ died for our sins, not our accidents or habits or hang-ups. We should call sin "sin," and accept that God, not us, decides what sin is and what it is not. We *rationalize* our sins when we find ways to keep on doing them because we have found an explanation or justification that lets us off the hook. It is like the young man that says, "I know the Bible says that sex outside of marriage is wrong, but Sara and I really love each other, so it is just like we are married except that we don't have this little piece of paper that says we are." He has taken truth "sex outside of marriage is wrong" and he has made up an argument so that the truth doesn't apply to him anymore.

God doesn't want us just acting like we are doing the right thing. He condemned the religious people of His day for cleaning the outside of the cup while the inside was filthy. He wants us to agree with Him *in our hearts.* If we don't let God do the hard work in our hearts, we will be forever weak Christians.

If you watch a butterfly as it struggles its way out of a cocoon, you may feel tempted to use a pair of scissors to help it out. Sticky strands of goo may seem to hold it back, yet the struggles of metamorphosis are necessary. Without the hindrances and the struggles to overcome them, the wings will never develop properly. If you help, you will produce a cripple, incapable of flight. Christians who have never known the hard work of repentance are like butterflies that will never been able to fly.

"What sorrow awaits you teachers of religious law and you
Pharisees. Hypocrites! For you are so careful to clean the outside
of the cup and the dish, but inside you are filthy—full of greed
and self-indulgence!" Matthew 23:25 (NLT)

DAY 92

Paul writes in Philippians 1:10-11, "For I want you to understand what really matters, so that you may live pure and blameless lives until the day of Christ's return. May you always be filled with the fruit of your salvation—the righteous character produced in your life by Jesus Christ—for this will bring much glory and praise to God."

I f you are really gifted, you may be tempted to coast through life without much effort. But in the area of our spiritual lives, that can be a big mistake. Some Christians act as if their gifting—whether it is healing or prophecy or miracles, or something else—qualifies them to never be questioned or held accountable. In the book of Romans, Paul says that we should not think more highly of ourselves than we ought. Another way to say that is, don't take yourself too seriously. If we depend on our gifting for our self-worth, to the exclusion of our character, we can end up looking like a beautiful tree with rotten fruit.

By now I'm sure you've heard about the moral failure of many Christian leaders in America. You may personally know someone, to everyone's surprise, whose secret sin has become public. We are shocked. How does this happen? Who would have thought that they even struggled with that sin?

Sins are like mushrooms; they grow best in the dark. It is dangerous to present a better image to those around us than what is really true. Like Paul says, don't think you are better than you really are. Being humble doesn't mean being a wimp; it is just being internally, ruthlessly, honest. And to have integrity means to be the same in public as you are in private.

It doesn't matter how gifted you are; if you've got cruddy character, it's like a gold ring in the snout of a pig.

DAY 93

People often complain that it's not fair that Adam and Eve sinned in the Garden of Eden and now we are held responsible for their sins. Why doesn't God let us start over every time so that we are accountable for our own? After all, isn't there a possibility that we might do it better than our first parents?

But the truth is pretty obvious. It's very much like two groups of people who go to war, and instead of having great battles with losses and wins, each side chooses to send out "their best man."

Adam and Eve were our best. They were in the perfect conditions that humans could find themselves in. They lived in Paradise and had everything at their disposal; even ruling over all the creatures on the earth. There was only one thing they couldn't do; eat of the tree of the knowledge of good and evil.

To not eat of that tree meant they had to trust God to tell them what was good and what was not. Instead, they allowed their experience to dictate that, and you and I know how that turned out.

Since they were in such a wonderful place, and had so little that they could not do, how can we assume we would do better? You can see the foolishness of that notion.

Most questions are good and have good answers that one can only find by digging more deeply with the expectation of finding the answer. C. S. Lewis said, "You can't go on 'seeing through' things forever. The whole point of seeing through something is to see something through it. To 'see through' all things is the same as not to see." — C.S. Lewis, *The Abolition of Man.*

But some questions don't matter much, so asking good questions is a great skill to acquire. It is like passengers sitting on the lower decks of the Titanic as she sank, arguing about whether or not she is an unsinkable ship. All bets are off when she begins to list forward and they can no longer sit or stand in peace. This is the situation we find ourselves in, we can realize the danger and do something about it or wait until it's too late.

DAY 94

P eople think that turning to Jesus will take all the fun out of life. But when you come to Jesus your capacity for joy is vastly increased. Sin only deadens us and saps our life, whereas Christ fills us with wonder and purpose.

G. Campbell Morgan tells of meeting as a boy an older man who had been converted to Christ through the ministry of his father. A few days after the man's conversion, Morgan encountered him in a garden. He was holding something small and was looking into his hand with a face full of wonder. Morgan asked him what it was, and with a voice filled with awe the man showed him a leaf that had fallen from a tree. "The beauty of God," he exclaimed. Even as an older man, he had been awakened to the wonder of life!

In contrast is the experience of Charles Darwin, the father of the theory of evolution. He turned his back on God and committed himself to secular humanism. His biography reveals that in so doing he lost his taste for life. As Darwin grew older, he admitted that he could no longer get anything out of poetry, music, or art. Life lost its flavor and he lived out his days in a world without wonder or joy.

The Bible is full of exclamations like: taste and see the Lord is good! The Joy of the Lord is our strength! The heavens declare the glory of God and the skies show His handiwork. The Lord has filled my heart with joy!

Sometimes we are like children who want to go on playing in mud puddles because we can't imagine what is meant by the offer of an ocean vacation.

"You make known to me the path of life; you will fill me with joy
in your presence, with eternal pleasures at your right hand."
Psalm 16:11 (NIV)

DAY 95

P eople who are not Christians cannot escape the power of sin. It is irresistible to them. But once you become a Christian, God gives you power over sin; you may still sin from time to time, but it is no longer irresistible; you have a choice. If I could use an analogy: Before you are a Christian, when you sin it is like getting stung by a hornet, and not only does it hurt you, but the venom of its sting poisons your body—Paul says that sin's sting is death—we die spiritually and are forever separated from God. When you become a Christian, you may sin, and it will hurt you (and others), but the venom is gone. The sting no longer results in death. The damage is limited, it hurts but doesn't kill.

Over time, you will lose your taste for sin. It is no longer as desirable as it once was. You find yourself living in the light of God's approval—and that is more fulfilling than all the sin you've ever done. You become one of God's kids—a part of His family—with the incredible inheritance of abundant life in this life, and eternal life after death.

Yet Christians will still struggle with sin. Somone once asked: "If you are bitten on the leg by a dog, would you beat your leg or beat the dog?"

The idea behind this is that when many Christians sin, they beat themselves. God has set us free from sin. When we sin, we should run to God, not away from Him, confessing our weakness and asking for the forgiveness that has been won through the cross. God is never surprised by our sin, and we should never be defeated by it.

"But when Christ had offered for all time a single sacrifice for sins, he sat down at the right hand of God," Hebrews 10:12 (ESV)

DAY 96

P eople will often talk about how important forgiveness is for the believer. It is true, believers must forgive others' their sins. Jesus talks about it clearly in the gospels:

"For if you forgive other people when they sin against you, your heavenly Father will also forgive you. But if you do not forgive others their sins, your Father will not forgive your sins." Matthew 6:14-15 (NIV)

That is some pretty serious stuff, and it is good to be reminded of how important forgiveness is every day. That's why Jesus taught His disciples to pray "and forgive us our sins as we forgive those who sin against us" in what is often called "The Lord's Prayer" or the "Our Father."

Yet, sometimes we need to forgive ourselves. It is pride that keeps us from forgiving others and pride that keeps us from forgiving ourselves. After all, if God Himself offers us forgiveness, who are we to stand in His way and say we can't forgive? We forgive because Christ has forgiven us.

Self-forgiveness is not about forgetting or dismissing our sins. It begins with acknowledging them, taking responsibility for what we have done, and then choosing to release the burden of guilt. 1 John 1:9 says that if we confess our sins, God forgives us. That applies to sins we commit; real humility begins with not having too exalted views of ourselves *and* not thinking too low of ourselves. We are a conundrum: we are God's treasure but still sinners even though we have been redeemed.

All forgiveness—forgiving and being forgiven—begins and ends at the cross. Philippians 2 says, "Who, being in very nature God, did not consider equality with God something to be used to His own advantage; rather, He made Himself nothing by taking the very nature of a servant, being made in human likeness. And being found in appearance as a man, He humbled Himself by becoming obedient to death—even death on a cross!" Part of following our Savior is following Him into death, our death to self, but then to get up and follow Him into His resurrected life.

Jesus, in great humility, did not seek the status of privilege but laid down His life to forgive us and save us. The sin of pride is the one thing that can keep us from it.

DAY 97

Psalms 103:13-14 reads: "As a father has compassion on his children, so the Lord has compassion on those who fear Him; for He knows how we are formed, He remembers that we are dust."

G od is not only merciful, but He is compassionate and understanding. He knows us. He is aware of our feelings, our weaknesses, and our inadequacies; and knowing them He enters into our experience and sympathizes with us. He is under no obligation to do so except for an obligation to His own nature. He would not be true to Himself if He did not enter into our experience with compassion and understanding. In this way He is also acting as a parent.

But we share an equal burden. Because we are understood, we must seek to understand. Because we are forgiven, we must show mercy. The measure of compassion we receive must be the measure of compassion we give.

There are times when we simply run out of steam. We pour ourselves out for others and yet they need even more. People don't seem to change. In our hurt we get to a point of caring only about our own pain. "What about me?" we ask in despair, feeling that our reservoir of compassion has been depleted. Yet we have a Father whose compassions never fail. To Him we must turn and drink compassion until our thirst is quenched, allowing His infinite fountains to wash over us.

We should think about God's compassion for us, thanking and praising Him even if we don't feel like it. It flows over us even when we cannot see it. It is in thanksgiving that our own dry wells fill once again. Psalm 87:7 "All my fountains are in You."

DAY 98

Remember when Jesus told Peter that Satan had asked to sift him as wheat. Jesus had just told them that one of them would betray Him, and they had gone from asking who that might be to arguing among themselves about which one of them is the greatest.

Even as believers, pride can be the darkness that connects us to Satan's underworld. We are no better than Peter or the rest of the disciples; we are capable of the same pride. But we should recognize that the areas where we hide our darkness contain our future defeat. We must be discerning of our own hearts. We must walk humbly with God and others.

There is nothing in the Bible that says that Satan can't still get permission to sift us like wheat. Wheat is sifted so the chaff can be thrown away. The chaff on wheat is a hard, husk-like covering that has no nutritional value and once it is separated from the wheat it is thrown away.

But it is good to know we have wheat in us. Sometimes God allows a satanic attack to clean us up: to get rid of our chaff; to cleanse our souls of darkness; to cleanse us of pride and greed and things that are opposed to His will. He wants to produce greater meekness and transparency in our lives. Our husk-like outer nature must die to facilitate the breaking forth of the wheat-like nature of Christ in us.

The greatest defense we can have against the devil is an honest, pliable heart before God. When the Holy Spirit puts His finger on an area of sin in our life, we must not run to defend ourselves.

"Surrender to God! Resist the devil, and he will run from you."
James 4:7 (CEV)

DAY 99

S atan's a liar and the father of lies.

Don Williams compares Satan's strategy to that of the Nazi concentration camp in Auschwitz, which has a sign in iron letters that reads "Work Makes You Free." Of course, it was a lie because there was no freedom, only work and the gas chambers. Williams says, "Again and again, Satan lifts up signs along the road to his gas chamber—signs that promise us freedom from the cycle of pain and shame. But there is only one true banner: 'Christ Is Freedom.' The devil wants to block this truth from our minds so that we remain docile, drugged, obedient, fantasy-fed, fantasy led and addicted subjects of his doomed kingdom."

It is a shame so many people buy into the devil's schemes through believing his lies. He is the definition of deception; the Scriptures even say he masquerades as an "angel of light". He was once an angel of light, but now is an angel of darkness reaping an existence cut off from the Creator of the universe and therefore devoid of light and love and peace and joy. There will be no laughter in hell, I'm pretty sure laughter will be one of the languages of Heaven. We often miss that solemn joy sometimes because our ideas of religion and holiness more often resemble sour pusses and unripe persimmons. But when Jesus greets the disciples returning from their mission, the Bible says in Luke 10 that He was "full of joy through the Holy Spirit". I like to think He danced a little jig.

Satan has tried to convince the world that religion and Christianity are the same. They are not. Religion is something that has been co- opted by the devil to make people miserable by making themselves the center of the universe. Religion is full of hypocritical, sad, and critical individuals who, while choking on the devil's lies, believe they are filled with God. They love to infect their church with darkness— and Jesus accused them of being just like their father. The devil.

So go on, chuckle a little. Love light and shun darkness.

DAY 100

"Shadrach, Meshach and Abednego replied to the king, 'O Nebuchadnezzar, we do not need to defend ourselves before you in this matter. If we are thrown into the blazing furnace, the God we serve is able to save us from it, and He will rescue us from your hand, O king. But even if He does not, we want you to know, O king, that we will not serve your gods or worship the image of gold you have set up.'" Daniel 3:16-18 (NIV)

So, we find ourselves timid about telling people about Jesus. We don't want to be embarrassed. We don't want to be seen as 'one of those people'. We don't want to put pressure on other people, because we don't want people to put pressure on us. If you will notice, all of these statements are about us and how we feel. None of them are about God.

If this is true about us, then we have to come to grips with the deep, deep crevice that exists between us and these young Jewish men. Not simply a distance of time, but a distance of focus and dedication and belief. Can we say we will stand with these young men and say, "God is able to save us, but even if He does not, we will never bow to another?" Can we say we will not bow to the culture; we will not bow to peer pressure; we will not bow to difficulty or hardship or embarrassment? And finally, can we say, we will not bow down to ourselves—to our comfort, to our pleasures, and to our sense of always trying to look good in front of others?

The folk-prophet Bob Dylan sang it truthfully, "But you're gonna have to serve somebody; it may be the devil, or it may be the Lord, but you're gonna have to serve somebody."

DAY 101

"For our struggle is not against flesh and blood, but against the rulers, against the authorities, against the powers of this dark world and against the spiritual forces of evil in the heavenly realms." Ephesians 6:12 (NIV)

S o, the question is, how do we keep ourselves pure? Pure not just morally, but pure in our thinking—pure about God and the world. We must become more militant in our battle, we must fight spiritually, fleshly. We must pray spiritually. Can you pray in the flesh? Absolutely. I hear soulish prayers all the time. If your prayers do not originate in the heart of God, then you are praying soulishly.

Our warfare, according to Paul, is spiritual—with unseen forces in the heavenlies. But the church has been on the defense too long. We must fight with everything we have. But how to fight is the question. Many take a cue from Daniel, where his prayers helped an angel get through the fight to answer his prayer. But it never says Dan addressed the principality; he prayed to God and God answered and the angels fought.

A soldier, whether a private or a General, will almost never engage the General of the opposing army. He will engage the foot soldiers of that army.

If you want to displace principalities, pray to God and engage the devil's foots soldiers and destroy the works of the devil. Cast out demons, heal the sick, save the lost. That's the battle and while it is not as flashy as addressing principalities, it is more effective for a foot soldier. (Romans 12:3 (NIV) says, "For by the grace given me I say to every one of you: "Do not think of yourself more highly than you ought, but rather think of yourself with sober judgment, in accordance with the faith God has distributed to each of you.") Stop caring what people may think about you. The warfare for us is here—in your mind and in your actions. Don't settle for soulish prayers—partner with God and His perfect will.

DAY 102

"So, you also should consider yourselves to be dead to the power of sin and alive to God through Christ Jesus." Romans 6:11 (NLT)

T he purpose behind Satan's realm is to ruin the Christian's life and therefore his testimony. Our faith conquers by clinging to eternal realities. So, what about when a Christian does not live this victory?

When you become a Christian, Paul says 'you are dead to sin and alive to Christ'. Dead here does not mean 'annihilated' but separated. Your 'sin factory' is still able to operate, and you still have access to it, but it doesn't run you. God's Spirit is now your new source of power to live by. Your will is free and is poised between the two sources; having the responsibility of refusing the call of the evil nature and heeding the urgings of the divine nature. The Christian never acts in a vacuum; he acts and speaks in the energy of the evil nature (the sin factory) or in the power of the divine nature (the Spirit within). There are things that feed the sin factory, and things that feed the divine nature. We become what we eat.

That's why we must live by the Spirit; we must give ourselves completely to God. We will either surrender ourselves to God, or surrender ourselves to sinful desires. There is no middle ground.

When you were born again, you became a sworn enemy to the legions of hell. If Satan and his minions cannot have your soul, they will settle for your reputation, your effectiveness, and your attention. They know that if you're not serving God, you're serving Satan.

If you don't live in victory, what do you do? Surrender yourself to God. And if you stumble, surrender. Don't run from God, run to Him. Then resist the demons and they will flee.

DAY 103

S ome of you today may be like Cornelius in Acts 10. You are a God fearer, but not a Christian. You go to church some, you pray, you try to live a moral life as best you can. I once knew a man in his 60's who had even served as a deacon in the church for years, but found out one day that he wasn't a Christian. He thought he was a Christian because he worked in the church, prayed, and tried to live a good life. But the Scriptures teach that living a good life is not enough; that even having a prayer life and giving to the poor and attending church does not make you a Christian any more than swimming in the ocean makes you a fish.

Christianity is about transformation; it is becoming a new person, not just taking a person and making them a little better. Jesus is the judge of all, and we must first settle our accounts with Him. We can't be good enough for God; He must come and make us good from the inside out. We can't be justified before God (made in right standing with Him) by being good and going to church. We need Jesus to make us okay with God. There must be time where we:

- Acknowledge our sinfulness before God
- Ask God to forgive all the wrong we've done and surrender our lives to Him—put Him in the 'drivers' seat'.
- We must acknowledge Jesus' death on the cross as payment for our sin and Jesus' resurrection from the dead as the power of a new life in God.
- And lastly, we must accept God's free gift of salvation and become filled with His life; the Holy Spirit of God.

Eternal life is not some place like a room we go into after we die. It is a person.

"We know also that the Son of God has come and has given us understanding, so that we may know Him who is true. And we are in Him who is true—even in His Son Jesus Christ. He is the true God and eternal life." 1 John 5:20 (NIV)

DAY 104

S urrender to God, resist the devil and he will flee from you...

Some people read the Bible a little, go to church sometimes, talk to God occasionally; but have not made a decision to follow Jesus. Maybe you've prayed the sinners' prayer—maybe you've prayed it a hundred times. But you still haven't come to a place where you are ready for God to take over every single part of your life. True salvation is trading your rights for God's ownership. As long as you are content to paddle around in the ocean, there's no need to grab a lifesaver. People don't die and go to hell because God doesn't love them; they die and go to hell because they refuse the only salvation that's offered them. Who would fault the captain of a ship if a passenger drowns because they refused to accept the lifesaver he threw to them? We can only be saved on God's terms, not ours. There's not one place in the Bible that lets us surrender only a portion of ourselves.

You don't get the experience of God's grace and mercy until you become willing to submit to it. Some have tried to get the benefit without the surrender and wonder why it doesn't work.

If you sit back and wait for it to make perfect sense before you dive in, you'll never take the plunge. It's like swimming. You can get all the information you want on the properties of water, on the physiology of the body in water—you can investigate until you exhaust every detail; but you'll never know that water can hold you up until you get in it. The same is true for God—without faith it is impossible to please Him; you gotta jump in the water.

"A man can eat his dinner without understanding exactly how food nourishes him. A man can accept what Christ has done without knowing how it works: indeed, he certainly would not know how it works until he has accepted it." — C. S. Lewis

DAY 105

"'Teacher, which is the most important commandment in the law of Moses?'" Jesus replied, 'You must love the Lord your God with all your heart, all your soul, and all your mind. This is the first and greatest commandment. A second is equally important: Love your neighbor as yourself.'" Matthew 22:36-39 (NLT)

W hy bother with relationships? Why can't we just be left alone rather than add something more to our already over-loaded lives? It is because relationships are the eternal part of our lives. Notice that the two greatest commands are not about being religious; they are about being relational. We were made to love God and each other. We are also called to be the objects of His love.

As we draw near to God—as we are caught up in his incredible, relentless love for us, the following will be true in our lives:

We'll no longer live for ourselves, but we will live to please Christ.

We'll not only love God, but we will love His people because He wants us to.

We'll realize we are called to be vulnerable. Christ gave His life up for us, so we also ought to give up our lives for others.

We'll find Christ's love for us has the potential to defeat our insecurities and give us the resources we need to love others. We love because He first loved us—and nothing can separate us from His love.

And lastly, we'll share in Jesus' wounds. 1 Peter 4:13 says: "But rejoice that you participate in the sufferings of Christ, so that you may be overjoyed when His glory is revealed." There is nothing wasted in the Kingdom of God; even our suffering is redeemed. As Brennan Manning says, "The unwounded life bears no resemblance to the Rabbi."

DAY 106

S trategy, methods, projects, and fundraising should never be the church's primary focus. Its' heartbeat is to nourish the life inside her that the world needs and craves. Marketing the church often leads to compromise and manipulation. Instead, she should compel, knowing that only the Holy Spirit can motivate believers to holiness, to service in the Kingdom, to selfless living and to lay down their lives for others and to love.

It can't be said any stronger than Scripture states it—the Church is called the Bride of Christ. When Jesus says the greatest command is this:

"Hear, O Israel, the Lord our God, the Lord is one. Love the Lord your God with all your heart and with all your soul and with all your mind and with all your strength" Mark 12:29-30 (NIV)

Yet we tend to treat it simply as words. Love is infinitely harder to "do" than "be good" or "work earnestly and hard". God wants a *love* relationship with us yet what we keep offering Him is duty, so that we can keep our heart and give it to other things. That is both wrong thinking and action. That is called idolatry.

The second command is to love our neighbor as ourselves. It takes supernatural love to genuinely love others. Our neighbors can be spiteful, greedy, lovers of themselves, sometimes hateful and even become our enemies, and we are sometimes that to our neighbors. We cannot love with supernatural, unstoppable, and selfless love unless we actually experience the love of the Father for ourselves. As the radiance and exact image of the invisible God, Jesus is a spiritual lover—our perfect and ultimate companion. Our first priority is to know Him in a passionate relationship with a love that is stronger than death. When love is stronger than death, then death loses its fearful hold on us and frees us to fully live—and to fully love our neighbors.

I am reminded of these words:

"Place me like a seal over your heart, like a seal on your arm; for love is as strong as death, its jealousy unyielding as the grave. It burns like blazing fire, like a mighty flame." Song of Songs 8:6 (NIV)

HOLY SPIRIT, MAKE US PASSIONATE LOVERS OF JESUS— WITH A LOVE THAT IS AS STRONG AS DEATH. AMEN

DAY 107

"And having disarmed the powers and authorities, he made public spectacle of them, triumphing over them by the cross." Colossians 2:15 (NIV)

The cross stands at the very heart of Christianity. Jesus came to die for us, not to give us some good ideas about God or living well. Christianity is not just another philosophy of life. Jesus used the reality of the cross to emphasize the need for absolute commitment to God and His Kingdom.

I hope most of you have seen "The Passion of Christ" movie. While we don't need to dwell on the graphic violence of the crucifixion, we must grasp the reality of Christ's suffering to truly appreciate what God accomplished through the cross. When we sanitize the cross—turning it into mere jewelry or decoration—we risk stripping it of its power. To understand what Jesus' death means for us, we need to reckon with the weight of his sacrifice, not reduce it to something comfortable or ornamental.

The Holy Spirit wants us to know the importance of Christ's sacrifice because the work of the cross should be central to our lives. The Bible hides nothing of the shame and grief that was involved for God's Son. How Jesus died is just as important as the fact of His death. The Old Testament prophecies concerning Christ's death put an emphasis on the details of His sufferings. If we feel the deep horror of the cross, we become more aware of the full extent of our sin. Calvary was not pretty. There was no sentiment in the Roman flogging. The Roman crucifixion has been universally recognized as being one of the cruelest forms of public execution ever devised. It was a horrible, slow, painful, and humiliating death. We more we see the depravity of our sin, the greater we will appreciate magnitude of God's love in Calvary.

DAY 108

"The expression of Christian character is not doing good, but God- likeness. If the Spirit of God has transformed you within, you will exhibit Divine characteristics. God's life in us expresses itself as God's life, not as human life trying to be godly." –Oswald Chambers

Many Christians I know want power, or glory, or wealth. Very few are as passionate about developing character. The problem with this line of thinking is that a person who possesses increasing power or glory or wealth and has a weakened character is in danger of becoming a rather soulless creature who lives by their appetites much like Esau in the Bible.

In his book, *The Abolition of Man*, Lewis was prophetic in pointing out that relativism—the idea that there are no absolute truths— would lead to the decay of morality and a lack of virtue within society. Without a belief in and the teaching of universal moral laws, we fail to educate the heart and are left with intelligent men who behave like animals or as Lewis puts it, "men without chests."

The head must rule the belly through the heart, or chest as Lewis says that what makes us truly human is the integration of all our parts. Our intellect alone would make us mere disembodied spirits; our appetites alone would reduce us to animals. The heart is what unites these dimensions, serving as the center of our character and identity.

Our emotions and heart require intentional discipline and training. They don't automatically become wise rulers over our minds and bodies the moment we surrender to Jesus. Instead, genuine transformation requires ongoing, disciplined training and complete dedication to becoming like Christ.

This isn't simply about forcing ourselves to "do good" through willpower. Rather, it's about the deep formation of our inner character—cultivating the kind of person we are becoming on the inside. Think of it as preparing a king to rule a kingdom: the heart must be properly trained and shaped so it can wisely govern the entire "kingdom" of our body, mind, and will. Our character, once formed, naturally directs our thoughts and desires rather than constantly battling against them.

A purity in your heart means no blend, no mixture. There is a single-minded devotion to Christ and to purity and holiness, a yearning after Him. There is only one master, one allegiance that our heart should follow. As the furnace of life is forged, true character will emerge inside us.

"Teach me Your ways, O Lord, that I may live according to Your truth. Grant me purity of heart, so that I may honor You." Psalm 86:11 (NLT)

DAY 109

T he female angler fish can grow up to 47 inches long, yet the male only grows up to 2.5 inches long. The male is rarely larger than a man's fist. These fish are found from 1600-10,000 feet deep in the Atlantic and Antarctic Oceans.

The male angler fish, when it is mature enough, connects itself to the female angler fish and is mated for life. It connects itself to the female with its teeth, and gets its nourishment for life from the female's blood stream. It completely depends on the female for nourishment, protection, and life. He literally has a grip for life.

Our life in God is much like that. He has made us so that when we "attach" ourselves to Him through Jesus Christ, we literally lose our lives into His. We may feel like at times we can barely hang on, but the truth is that He gives us a grip for life—nothing can separate us from the love of God in Christ Jesus.

Christians are often found arguing about the "once saved, always saved" and the "you can lose your salvation" perspectives. I see both sides biblically. But I find it really hard to be dogmatic because there is simply no way for us to know, with certainty, whether or not someone is "saved." If they "lose" their salvation, was it because they never really had it? Or what about those who subscribe to "once saved, always saved," yet live their lives practicing all kinds of ungodly things believing that one profession of faith would keep them in good standing with God no matter what they might do? It is a big issue—much larger than I could address here.

But this I do know, and it makes sense to me: If Jesus has me in His grip, and I don't fight against Him, then I can rest safely "in His grip." After all, Jesus Himself is called "eternal life!"

"And we know that the Son of God has come, and He has given us understanding so that we can know the true God. And now we live in fellowship with the true God because we live in fellowship with

His Son, Jesus Christ. He is the only true God, and He is eternal
life." 1 John 5:20 (NLT)

So, the best and surest bet for all of us is to stay intimately connected to Jesus Christ by faith. You want assurance of salvation? Then there is no safer place in the galaxies than to be securely in the grip of the Lord Jesus Christ, wherever He goes, we go! And on the less serious side, we all get to wear our "I'm with Him" t-shirts. Forever.

DAY 110

T he first thing that goes away when we are hurt in a relationship is trust. But if it takes time to build trust, it takes even more time to rebuild trust. I Corinthians 13:7 says,

"Love always protects, always trusts, always hopes, always perseveres." It never gives up. In verse four, it says, "love is patient."

So, if you want to give up, and if you can't be patient, maybe your problem is a lack of love. Perhaps you have confused need with love. It is true that we all basically love because we need to be loved, but as God pours out His love in our hearts, He transforms us and a little of His "otherly" love—what the Bible calls Agape love—gets placed in our hearts. You might need more of His love in you.

"And hope does not disappoint us, because God has poured out His love into our hearts through the Holy Spirit, whom He has given us." Romans 5:5 (MSB)

And maybe along the freeway of life you have begun to lose you trust in God. Psalm 145:13 says, "The Lord is faithful to all His promises and loving toward all He has made."

Perhaps you don't think He is loving toward all He has made. Life can be very difficult. God will allow hard things to come your way in order to share in His holiness. But if you've gotten hardened by life's toughness and you don't trust God anymore; you need to start with repentance; that is, take God at His word. Believe what He says about Himself.

There are people in the Bible who suffered more than you and still continued to trust God and praise His loving kindness. This may seem like a harsh thing to you, but it is about faith. God is not defined by our circumstances. God is not defined by our experiences or lack thereof. He defines Himself in Scripture as long-suffering, patient, kind, loving, honest and trustworthy. That is where we find out the truth about who God is.

DAY 111

T he Kingdom of God is what things would be like if Jesus ran everything and if His will was done everywhere. The Kingdom of God is what things would be like if Jesus was in charge.

A great secret is revealed as Jesus came to the earth to establish an outpost of the Kingdom of God. Jesus talks about this in two stages. In the first stage the Kingdom is hidden; it is not obvious. You have to look for it and seek it out.

But in the second stage, the Kingdom will be more obvious and out front. It is going to be staggering and immense, like a nuclear explosion. In that first stage there is invitation and God doesn't displace everyone's will. In the first stage, God's will is done but is also allowed to be thwarted because He allows the will of mankind and Satan to be done.

The second stage is the physical coming (return) of Jesus to the earth to set up the physical Kingdom of God on earth. When He returns, there will be only one will done on earth—the will of God.

But now, today, God's will can be ignored, resisted, or thwarted. That is the mystery of the Kingdom. It is here (but not permanently or physically), and it is the future. That's why we must constantly pray for the Kingdom to come, it will not be fully come until Jesus physically returns to earth.

So, God's future Kingdom, where healing and justice and love will reign supreme for all time, was brought into the present through Jesus' ministry. God's rule and reign came as Jesus proclaimed the good news of God's plan to crush the works of Satan, and was demonstrated by healing the sick, casting out demons, raising the dead, offering forgiveness, extending compassion and delivering the oppressed.

So pray with me, "Lord, may Your Kingdom come and Your will be done on earth as it is in Heaven. Amen"

DAY 112

"The Kingdom of Heaven is like treasure hidden in a field. When a man found it, he hid it again, and then in his joy went and sold all he had and bought that field." Matthew 13:44 (NIV)

A treasure buried in a field worth a great price, but we must dig through the dirt to get to it. Dan Allender says, "As human beings we are common dirt given life by the breath of God. We see, smell, taste, touch, and hear God in a creation that bears His intimate mark but cannot contain the glory that awaits. God leaves sensual traces of Himself everywhere: in fine chocolate and a great burger, in a Bach fugue and wail of Jimi Hendrix, in the waft of barbecued ribs and fresh breeze off the sea. A radical life grasps both the weariness of this soiled world and its capacity to transfix us with God's glory...A radical life is one that knows the world is soiled and smeared in toil. Yet grandeur pulses through the ecosystem, freshness rises, and the Spirit sings if one merely has the eyes and ears to hear. A radical life has eyes and ears for the deepest purposes of God."

Our problem is that we have such a hard time being so passionate only for God. We find our pleasures elsewhere, not realizing they are but shadowy substitutes for the reality of HIM. We don't treasure the treasure; we need God's assistance. What is often most broken in us is our "want to."

I've had many people say to me, "I want to believer, and I just can't". I have always responded with, "belief is a choice, if you wait for complete understanding, you will never believe because you are making your understanding 'god'. That's why Jesus never says, understand me and be saved. Instead, He says, believe on me and live forever.

"Martha," Jesus said, "You don't have to wait until then. I am the Resurrection, and I am Life Eternal. Anyone who clings to me in faith, even though he dies, will live forever. And the one who lives by believing in me will never die. Do you believe this?" John 11:25-26 (TPT)

But what God does for us, He does in us. He will help us to "treasure the treasure." When we are motivated, we will move mountains to find it. Join with me in this prayer— "God give us, above all else, that one true desire for Your Kingdom. Show us our poverty—and make us desperate for You."

DAY 113

"The Lord is close to the brokenhearted; He rescues those whose spirits are crushed." Psalms 34:18 (NLT)

R emember the life of Joseph? Rejected by his own brothers—falsely accused by his employer; thrown into jail. Forgotten. Eventually redeemed, becomes the number two man in Egypt and runs into his family. Treats them all well, gives them good jobs and places to live.

Then there is young David—anointed King over Israel by Samuel. Later Saul tried twice to put a spear through him. Finally, Saul puts out a hit on David who then runs for his life for about ten years.

So, what do these guys have in common? They were treated very badly by close relatives, or fellow 'believers', or spiritual fathers. "So what?" you may say. Well, that's not all they have in common; they were not only wounded, but they seemed to be able to rise above unforgiveness, bitterness and self-pity and live their lives unencumbered by the past.

How did they do that? What do we do with the wounds we get from others? What about the wounds from relatives or Christians and sometimes even Christian leaders?

The thing is neither David nor Joseph ever saw themselves as simply in the hands of people. They were in the Hands of God, and therefore the wounds and sins that came from others did not debilitate them.

We are never at the mercy of anyone who might hurt us; we are in the hands of God. The remedy for hurt is not to say "Christians, especially leaders, should never sin against us." The remedy is: "Christians, and sometimes leaders, may sin against us; but we can, like David and Joseph, commit ourselves to being in God's hands." After all, He is close to the brokenhearted.

DAY 114

"The Lord now chose seventy-two other disciples and sent them
ahead in pairs to all the towns and places He planned to visit."
Luke 10:1 (NLT)

J esus trained the disciples with a show and tell model; or more
accurately—a tell and show model. He went out and proclaimed the
good news, healed the sick, cast out demons, and raised the dead— all
while His disciples watched.

Jesus then sent out first the twelve, then the seventy-two with instructions
to do what He did.

So, the model was: Listen to what Jesus said, watch what Jesus did; then go
do that to others: tell and show.

The beautiful thing about Jesus' training was that it was not based in
technique (five steps to casting out demons, or three steps to healing); it
was based in relationship. They lived with Jesus, slept beside Him, and ate
meals together; three years of intimate relationship. And out of that
relationship—listening to Jesus and watching Him do the stuff—they began
to sound a little like Him and look a little like Him.

What it means to be a Christian today is the same as then: we are followers
of Christ who are to go tell and show. If you think you've been slighted
because Jesus is not physically present with us as He was with the early
disciples, think again. We have the added bonus of the Holy Spirit of Jesus
living inside of us.

And if for some reason you think that only the twelve Apostles were called
to the tell and show model—remember that this verse in Luke tells us that
Jesus sent out not only the twelve, but also the seventy- two. The tell and
show model is for every follower of Christ.

DAY 115

T he responsibilities of our life together, what we call Church, have often been taught as unromantic; it is disciplined obedience to the Great Commission. Whether or not it is teaching Sunday School, helping in the nursery, greeting at the front door, serving coffee to guests, making or bringing meals, giving our time, energy and money—it is believed that if we just do our duty, fill our slots, we will be happy—or at least happy if someone else does it for us. It is thought that prayer is too hard, feelings are irrelevant, and getting the job done is the only thing that counts.

Many Christians believe that we don't need spiritual experience to proclaim the Gospel, so they have no expectation of God's immediate presence with us; there is no sense that intimacy with God is normal. As a result, much of the church today can function without His manifest Presence.

The prophet says this, "You will seek me and find me when you seek me with all your heart." Jeremiah 29:13 (NIV) We've gone through enough of the misery of life to know that without actually finding God, we cannot do, or hope to do, any ministry. We believe that God meets our desperation—if we have not found God then we have not sought Him with all our hearts.

That is part of what God is doing; He is driving us into His arms through divine desperation. It is much like what Moses says in Deuteronomy:

"He humbled you, causing you to hunger and then feeding you with manna, which neither you nor your fathers had known, to teach you that man does not live on bread alone but on every word that comes from the mouth of the Lord." Deuteronomy 8:3 (NIV)

LORD, MAKE US DESPERATE WITH HUNGER, THEN FEED US WITH THE ONLY BREAD THAT SATISFIES...YOUR SON, JESUS CHRIST.

DAY 116

T he unkind word or forgetful lapse of sensitivity appear to be either a minimal offense given what we may be capable of, or actually acceptable if one were to see the world from our vantage point. Contempt is most often hidden behind "they deserve my contempt or rage" because of how they have acted. It excuses the sin of rage and degrading or demeaning others through feeling that they are reasonable and justifiable.

The part of shame that lies beneath my contempt has more to do with not being humiliated. The idea that I am not smart enough, or adequate enough (whatever the task), reinforces my deepest fears. I keep my head low knowing I am not the smartest guy in the room, but I keep it above the heads of lesser mortals, usually by demeaning others who might be as or more competent than me.

We sang a song called "Joy" in church when I was young. It says, "Jesus, others and you, what a wonderful way to spell joy." We seem to have lost that kind of innocent truth, thinking that we don't love ourselves enough and that is why we feel so lousy. The reality is that God knows that when we put ourselves first, it will always make us feel lousy, and will lead to all kinds of misdeeds, some of them not as bad as contempt, but all of them damaging to those around us.

The scriptural precedent is to love God with absolute abandon, and love your neighbor as yourself. Jesus knew that one of our most flagrant flaws is loving ourselves—Adam and Eve were tempted in the garden by Satan's crafty statement "your eyes will be opened, and you will be like God, knowing good and evil", and were convinced that being equal with God is worth disobedience to Him.

When I am finding fault with others and not exercising love, I am acting in contempt, and that eats away at both our hope and our longings. We long to be love, we hope to be loved in the way that God really loves us. The lie, just like in the garden, is that God is not to be trusted and we should be the ones who decides what is right and wrong. We are shamed from the beginning and if we don't accept God's healing forgiveness, we will live out that shame in contempt of God and man.

DAY 117

The work of these evil spirits on people in the church is described in Jude:

> "These men are grumblers and faultfinders; they follow their own evil desires; they boast about themselves and flatter others for their own advantage...These are the men who divide you, who follow mere natural instincts and do not have the Spirit." Jude 1:16-19 (NIV)

The basis for the enemy's attack is Satan's character—in Revelation 12:10 he is called "the accuser of the brethren." One way this spirit operates is to encourage believers to find fault in one another.

> "You should know this, Timothy, that in the last days there will be very difficult times. For people will love only themselves and their money. They will be boastful and proud, scoffing at God, disobedient to their parents, and ungrateful. They will consider nothing sacred. They will be unloving and unforgiving; they will slander others and have no self-control. They will be cruel and hate what is good. They will betray their friends, be reckless, be puffed up with pride, and love pleasure rather than God. They will act religious, but they will reject the power that could make them godly. Stay away from people like that!" 2 Timothy 3:1-5 (NLT)

The faultfinder spirit's assignment is to assault relationships on all levels. It pits children against parents, husbands against wives, members against members, and members against leaders, seeking to bring irreparable divisiveness into the church.

Masquerading as discernment, this spirit will slip into our opinions of other believers, leaving us critical and judgmental. As one prophetic person liked to say, a religious spirit traffics in legalism, opinion, debate, judgment and criticism. Consequently, we all need to evaluate our attitude toward others. If our thoughts are other than faith working through love, we need to be aware that we may be under spiritual attack.

Chaos and discord are Satan's playground; peace and love is the atmosphere of Heaven.

DAY 118

> "Then Jesus, full of the Holy Spirit, returned from the Jordan River. He was led by the Spirit in the wilderness, where He was tempted by the devil for forty days." Luke 4:1-2 (NLT)

Full of the Holy Spirit; led by the Spirit. We think that in that state Jesus would be led to preach a great revival—or maybe heal an entire village—or miraculously feed thousands from a few fish and biscuits.

But Jesus full of the Spirit is led (in the Greek it is literally 'driven') by the Spirit to be tempted for forty days by the devil. This perhaps exposes some of our misconceptions about how things work in the world.

We often associate the fullness of the Spirit with a demonstration of God's power; like healing or evangelism or miracles. Or often associate being led by the Spirit as God taking us to some great assignment—like a divine appointment or even the mission field.

So here are a few observations. Number one, the devil is a formidable enemy. While we should not fear him, we should also not be naive about his power. Secondly, God may fill us with His Spirit in order for us to be able to stand against temptation. Thirdly, God may lead us into the wilderness.

Remember that you need God's power to resist the devil and to stand against temptation. Remember that God sometimes empowers us not so that we can be God's man or woman for the hour, but so that we can trek out across the desert of our circumstances, not losing faith and come out victorious on the other side.

So, when you find yourself spitting sand and feeling the heat of an unmerciful sun, just remember God's power is available to us even if it just the power to help us hang on a little while longer and not give up. You'll be glad you did.

DAY 119

"Then someone called from the crowd, 'Teacher, please tell my brother to divide our father's estate with me.'" Luke 12:13 (NLT)

T his man connects to a universal human impulse—the desire for justice. Jesus responds to the man's demand by questioning his motives. Is greed or justice behind the demand?

Here Jesus uses a story to answer the man's question. First you have a rich man…in a society where the rich are the recipients of God's blessing. But the man doesn't see his wealth as a blessing—it is a problem to be addressed: 'What am I to do with all this extra grain? I'll build bigger barns.'

He doesn't see himself as a steward of what God has given him— 'what does God want me to do with this excess?' Instead, he sees himself as a self-made man. He earned it. He can decide how to use it. He has a problem, not an opportunity. He presumes to be in control.

The crops seem more than sufficient for him and his family. He never thinks of the poor as a 'solution.' He never even consults another person. He is the god of his own little fiefdom.

This is the greedy man. Aristotle once remarked that the surest way to destroy someone was to give the person his own way. If there is no God, then there will be no accounting when we die. We can build bigger barns, feed our greed and be selfish and self-determined and then die, and that would be it. But if God exists, then He says there will be an accounting. And anyone who, in their greed, only stores up treasures in this life and has no eternal bank account will find themselves bankrupt in the life to come.

All that we have belongs to God. Let's honor Him by how we handle it. Our high calling is to be stewards of God's Kingdom.

DAY 120

"Then the angel spoke to the women. 'Don't be afraid!' he said. 'I know you are looking for Jesus, who was crucified. He isn't here! He is risen from the dead, just as He said would happen. Come, see where His body was lying.'" Matthew 28:5-6 (NLT)

God, in Jesus, chose the path of weakness over power. The cross defines God as One who is willing to relinquish power for the sake of love. Power without mercy, tends to cause suffering. Love, being vulnerable, absorbs it. On a hill called Calvary, God renounced power for the sake of love.

So, what difference does it make that Jesus suffered such shame, humiliation and death? The resurrection is the difference. Can you think of someone you were once close to who has died? What would it mean for you if that person actually rose from the dead? If, in utter astonishment, you found yourself facing this person again—what would that be like?

That image in your mind is a hint of what the disciples felt on that resurrection morning. They had grieved for three days. Suddenly, hope rose in their hearts. Could it be? Could God, against all odds, reverse the irreversible?

The early church hung everything on the resurrection. Paul told the Corinthian church, in I Corinthians 15:14, that "if Christ has not been raised, our preaching is useless and so is your faith". The resurrection is the main event. If you don't believe Jesus rose from the dead, you are not a believer at all.

I think it may have been C. S. Lewis who said that the Son of God became a man to enable us to become children of God. By His death, our sin was accounted for, and by His resurrection our new life can begin. Christ is risen; He is risen indeed!

DAY 121

"This is real love—not that we loved God, but that he loved us and sent his Son as a sacrifice to take away our sins." 1 John 4:10 (NLT)

T his is love: not that we loved God, but that He loved us and sent His Son as an atoning sacrifice for our sins. "Atoning sacrifice" here means "mercy seat;" it is the same as the Old Testament word atonement, meaning "to cover." In the tabernacle in the Holy of Holies there was the Ark of the Covenant. On top of that ark there was a lid topped with two cherubim of gold, facing each other and looking down on the lid of the box. That lid was called the mercy seat. Only once a year, the high priest came into the Holy of Holies, bringing blood to be sprinkled on the mercy seat. The priest, representing the people, met with God. But they had to do it God's way. God loved them, but He didn't simply slosh over with love and say, "You can come to Me any way you want." This was the way they were to come to God, and only that way.

The Lord Jesus Christ is called "the atoning sacrifice for our sins" which means that He is the mercy seat for our sins. Jesus is Himself the mercy seat because He died on earth for us -- Jesus, our Lord, was handed over to death because of our failures and was brought back to life so that we could receive God's approval.

He has made atonement for our sins so that you and I can come with boldness to God's throne of grace. But we have to do it God's way— through Jesus' Sacrifice. That throne is now a throne of grace because there is mercy there for us. That is what Christ did, and that is the way God demonstrated His love for us.

DAY 122

"This is what God told us: God has given us eternal life, and this life is in His Son. Whoever has the Son has life, but whoever does not have the Son of God does not have life." 1 John 5:11-12 (NCV)

It is not uncommon for believers of Christ to struggle with thoughts like, "maybe I'm just not good enough to be a Christian," or "nothing really happened to me when I gave my life to Christ, nothing has really changed." But Christianity is more than jumping off a cliff in the dark hoping there is something to land on. It is a personal relationship with the God of the universe. The assurance of your relationship with God is based on the authority of the Bible, God's Word, not on how you feel.

It is much like flying in an airplane. You may be flying completely upside down in a fog and feel like you are right-side up. Only the instrument panel can tell you the truth. A pilot must trust his instrument panel rather than his senses. The same is true for a Christian. We must trust, that is—have faith, based upon the Word of God. God's Word is our instrument panel and we rely upon it and not our feelings.

So, when the enemy comes and whispers to you, "you're not good enough" or "you'll never measure up;" don't argue with him. In fact, you can say. "You're right, I'm not good enough, and I'll never measure up. Jesus is my goodness and He has measured up for me. I belong to Him. If you have a problem with me, I'd suggest you take it up with my Master. Now I'm done talking to you, goodbye."

It's why Jesus used words of Scripture to rebuke the devil in the wilderness. The temptations all had to do with how Jesus felt. Since you are hungry, make bread. Since you desire the kingdoms of the world, bow down to me. Since you want to show everyone that you are the Messiah, throw yourself off this Temple. Of course, the devil was just guessing how Jesus felt by projecting his own weaknesses upon Him. But Jesus answered with The Truth. When the Bible says you are a child of God, you can put all your weight into that regardless of how you feel today.

DAY 123

"This same Good News that came to you is going out all over the world. It is bearing fruit everywhere by changing lives, just as it changed your lives from the day you first heard and understood the truth about God's wonderful grace." Colossians 1:6 (NLT)

T he power of the gospel is changed lives. Jesus said that we would know people by the fruit of their lives—grapevines produce grapes; apple trees apples. In other words, the kind of change that the gospel brings to us is a change that begins inside and works its way out.

We are called to be Christian, not religious. To be religious means to hide behind a veneer of religion; it is putting on a show. Jesus accused the Pharisees of this when they wanted everyone to think they were better than they really were. On the outside they looked all pious and holy, but on the inside they were full of greed, self-indulgence, hypocrisy and wickedness.

The gospel of Christ changes us from the inside out. We begin to bear fruit that is more in keeping with God's desires for us. But an apple tree doesn't strive to bear fruit. It doesn't moan and groan and sweat and struggle to grow apples; it produces them naturally.

That is the kind of change that the gospel brings. It isn't a change we have to put on, or moan and groan and strain to get; it is a natural result of our surrender to the Holy Spirit of God that He put in us when we first believed.

Our constant prayer should be,

"Lord change me on the inside; and help me not fake it while you're doing it. Make me a good tree, Lord."

Meditative Reflection

The Welsh Revival of 1904–1905 is one of the most striking examples of how the gospel can transform not just individual lives, but entire communities. I am most moved by the stories of the coal miners. These men were known for their roughness—long days underground, harsh conditions, and coarse language were simply part of their world. Cursing was not just a habit; it was the soul of the mines themselves.

But when the revival swept through Wales, something remarkable happened. Men who had never once bowed their heads in prayer were suddenly weeping under conviction. Hardened faces softened. Families were restored. Taverns emptied, jails emptied, sports events ceased, prayer meetings overflowed, and hymns echoed down the streets where shouting once did. Yet the detail that always captures my heart is this: the transformation was so real, so inward, that the miners no longer spoke as they once did. The pit ponies—who pulled the coal carts—had grown used to responding to curses and harsh commands. When the men were changed, their tongues changed too. Their words no longer carried the sharp, cutting force they once did. The ponies did not know how to obey commands without curse words in them. The entire mining system had to adjust to the newfound grace and peace in the hearts of the workers.

DAY 124

"To escape the error of salvation by works we have fallen into the opposite error of salvation without obedience. In our eagerness to get rid of the legalistic doctrine of works we have thrown out the baby with the bath and gotten rid of obedience as well." - A.W. Tozer

M y mom's family took baths on their back porch, sharing the same bathwater in in a horse trough. The first to take a bath was the father, secondly the mother, followed by all the children and finally the baby was last. That means that for mom's family, six people took their bath before the baby, and by that time the water was murky and it would have been easy to throw the baby out with the dirty water by mistake.

The phrase "throwing the baby out with the bathwater" comes from an old German proverb, "Das Kind mit dem Bad ausschütten." The idea is that one should avoid getting rid of something valuable along with the undesirable parts of a situation.

Historically, in the past, when people bathed less frequently, entire families would use the same bathwater. By the end of the process, the water would be quite dirty. The proverbial warning was to be careful not to discard the baby along with the dirty water, highlighting the risk of losing something important while trying to get rid of something undesirable.

The expression reflects a caution against making hasty decisions that might lead to unnecessary loss or the removal of something valuable in the process of eliminating the negative aspects of a situation.

DAY 125

T o move toward authenticity requires real courage; it requires turning from our selfish ways; our self-protection, our self- determination, and our self-centeredness.

Take a minute and think of the three most important relationships in your life, such as those with a spouse or family member or close friends or even business associates. How many of you know that you are settling for false community with at least one of those three people?

We settle for false community instead of demanding the real thing usually because of one thing: fear. We ask: What if airing the issue actually makes things worse? What if exploring the situation more only serves to ruin the relationship? If I were really honest, can the relationship survive?

To these fears, and even more, there is only one response: the black hole. As scary as that is, those who enter the black hole of fear are the ones most likely to pop up one day into the fresh, life-giving daylight of genuine community.

Imagine with me just a glimpse of authentic community. We aren't trying to fix each other. We have genuine compassion for each other and we don't compete with each other. We may disagree but we refuse to draw blood. We have the freedom to talk to each other about how we really feel.

We are moving against our base impulse to protect ourselves; we are pushing through our fear into what feels like uncharted territory. But it is charted. We have one who has gone before us. Christ Himself loved us first, chose to die for us while we were still sinners, and has promised to live in us by His Holy Spirit to empower us to follow Him into the dark tunnel of fear and into the light.

DAY 126

"Unless the Lord builds the house, its builders labor in vain."
Psalms 127:1 (NIV)

No one could have guessed that years ago the world trade center would disappear from the New York Skyline. We seem to be threatened at every hand with impermanence. Things that we thought would last don't. Job security is constantly threatened—if not from layoffs and shutdowns, then from disaster or drought.

George Boschke was the famous engineer who built the gigantic sea wall to protect Galveston, Texas from floods that had brought disaster to the city. From Galveston he went to Oregon to build railroads in an undeveloped section of the state. Boschke was in a camp forty miles away from the nearest railroad when an exhausted messenger rode in and handed a telegram to his assistant. The message said that the Galveston Sea wall had been washed away by a furious hurricane. The assistant dreaded handing the telegram to his boss. Boschke read the telegram, smiled, handed it back and said, "This telegram is a black lie. I built that wall to stand."

He turned and walked away and went about his work. It turned out that the message was based on a false report. True, there had been a hurricane as severe as that which had blooded the city before, but Boschke's sea wall had not been moved. It stood firm. "I built that wall to stand," said Boschke and went smiling about his work amid rumors of disaster.

God is determined to grow character in us. He does this through adversity and pain. Character is forged in the fires of life, not on the mountaintop. God want to build a life of permanence. He wants to be able to say of us, "I built that life to stand."

DAY 127

We are living in times of deep uncertainty. People are losing jobs, institutions we once trusted feel compromised, and many sense an uneasy pressure—an almost gnawing fear—that something is not well in America and that we may be heading toward some kind of breaking point. In moments like these, we naturally turn to God. But **how** we turn to Him is of ultimate and eternal importance.

Picture God as an ocean. Our endless temptation would be to walk down to the shoreline—to splash around, but careful not to swim, not to dive, to never venture beyond our depth—desperately clinging tightly to a lifeline connecting us to our ordinary, comfortable life. We search for the minimum that will be accepted. We want to be safe.

We're like honest but reluctant taxpayers: we approve of income tax in principle and file truthfully, but we dread any increase. We want to give God something, but are constantly looking for loopholes to help us be better keepers than givers. We are meticulous about paying no more than necessary.

The lie we tell ourselves is that our best protection comes from guarding our money, our habitual comforts, and our ambitions—perhaps even asking God to protect these things for us. This is simply false.

In this life, we are called to *expend* our lives, not save them. Our real protection lies elsewhere: in our relationship with Jesus. And that protection isn't about our possessions—it's about *us*.

Swimming lessons are better than a lifeline to shore. That lifeline is actually a death line, creating the illusion of permanent security. When it's gone, we drown. But the lessons save us. We are called to "swim in Him."

Our life in God isn't about giving "just this much" time or "this much" attention. It's not even about giving all our time and attention. **God wants us.** All of us John the Baptist's words are true for every believer: "He must increase, and I must decrease." God is infinitely merciful to our repeated failures—but there is no promise that He will bless a deliberate compromise.

What matters—what Heaven desires and hell fears—is precisely that further plunge: diving deeper into waters beyond our control, abandoning ourselves utterly, completely, and absolutely to God.

We lose our lives to gain His.

"Whoever tries to keep their life will lose it, and whoever loses their life will preserve it." Luke 17:33 (NIV)

DAY 128

"Therefore, my dear friends, as you have always obeyed—not only in my presence, but not much more in my absence—continue to work out your salvation with fear and trembling." Philippians 2:12

Spiritual growth is not automatic; it must be intentional. It requires commitment and effort to grow. Character is shaped by the habits we develop, and we do not automatically develop good habits, even as Christians.

Spiritual growth is a process that takes time, it does not happen overnight and it will not happen without real commitment and effort. And it is true that spiritual maturity is demonstrated more by our behavior than our beliefs. That is what James was trying to communicate in his Biblical letter: real belief has feet; it is tangible and looks like something more than just mental assent. We also know that Christians need relationships with other Christians in order to grow.

We can't really grow in isolation—it is the friction (iron sharpens iron) with other believers and their encouragement that helps us grow. And not just encouragement, but we must live in the tension of loving our brothers and sisters in the Lord even when they don't act in a way that we like. It takes a variety of spiritual experiences with God to produce spiritual maturity. Gene Getz said, "Bible study by itself will not produce spirituality. In fact, it will produce carnality if it isn't applied and practiced." You can surely see that in the life of the Pharisees in Scripture. Study without service produces Christians with judgmental attitudes and spiritual pride. When Christians began to back-bite and turn on each other, it usually means that they no longer are throwing themselves into Jesus' cause in the world; they are no longer ministering to others. They've somehow decided to just take time off as they indulge in feeding themselves while refusing to give themselves away to others.

Christianity is primarily about relationships with God and with others. We must put into practice all that we learn; that is discipleship.

And without that application and practice, we will never grow into maturity. Christianity is a matter of the head and the heart. It is also a matter of being who we say we are so that the witness of our lives is not just words, but actions.

DAY 129

"We loved you so much that we shared with you not only God's Good News but our own lives, too." 1 Thessalonians 2:8 (NLT)

W e are often warned about Christian leaders. "Watch out, they only want your money! They only care about numbers, not people." And all our suspicions about them are deepened with every report of a Pastor who embezzled, or who had an affair, or who misused authority.

So, during my lifetime there has been a steady rise in "accountability." It seems to be the new catchword—we have accountability partners, accountability web sites, and even accountability groups. The problem with accountability is that it is voluntary—it only works to the extent that people are honest, transparent and forthcoming about their life.

This can be a hardship for Christian leaders, especially pastors. Many of them have been hurt as they opened their hearts and their lives. Sometimes their confidences are betrayed. Sometimes self-appointed healers want to fix them, or people think they could do a much better job than the leader.

When Christian leaders train God's people, they cannot limit themselves to weekly sermons, prayer meeting and occasional conferences or outreaches. Training in godliness must be well- rounded. No matter what the cost, it must include love, example and vulnerability. Paul wrote to the Thessalonians that he and Silas and Timothy were ready to share with them not only the gospel, but their own lives too. A leader's whole life needs to be on view and available to those he wants to help follow Christ more closely. Paul says "Imitate me as I imitate Christ." 1 Corinthians 11:1 (GW)

If you are a leader in Christ's Church, you must press in to share not only your gifts—whether teaching, preaching, or leading—you must also press in to share your very life. Just be prepared to share in the sufferings of Christ as you do.

DAY 130

hat if all that your life is built on is a lie?

"Satan has blinded the minds of unbelievers." 2 Corinthians 4:4 (NIV)

What if the one who created you desires to be with you forever, but there is an enemy who wants to keep that from happening? The choice is yours.

"No one can separate us from the love of God in Jesus Christ" and "He is not willing that any should perish." Romans 8:39 & 2 Peter 3:9

What if the truth has been mocked and derided so much all your life that you are now desensitized to it? "No knowledge of the truth." "Black is white, and white is black." 2 Timothy 3:7 & Isaiah 5:20

What if the devil was not some silly red beast with a pointed tail and pitchfork; what if he looks more like the wealthiest and wisest among us? "Even Satan disguises himself as an angel of light." "He is the god of this age." 2 Corinthians 11:14 & 2 Corinthians 4:4

WHAT IF THE DEVILS' PLAN HAS ALWAYS BEEN TO ENSLAVE HUMANITY AND KEEP THEM FROM GOD?

"For freedom Christ has set us free; stand firm therefore, and do not submit again to a yoke of slavery." Galatians 5:1

What if the blue pill means more in Christianity than in the Matrix? In The Matrix, the main character Neo is offered the choice between a red pill and a blue pill by rebel leader Morpheus. The red pill represents an uncertain future—it would free him from the enslaving control of the machine-generated dream world and allow him to escape into the real world, but living the "truth of reality" is harsher and more difficult. On the other hand, the blue pill represents a beautiful prison. "For the wages of sin is death, but the gift of God is eternal life through Jesus Christ our Lord." Romans

6:23 (NIV) The red pill means accepting Christ and giving your life to Him—leading to eternal life; but that choice in this life will be harsher and more difficult. The blue pill keeps you in soul sleep and is a pleasant way to live thinking you are free from rules and restrictions. But in the end, it leads to eternal death, or hell as it has been called.

What if the devil has deceived the human race because he is jealous of our relationship with God and doesn't want us reconciled with our creator? Jesus said,

---

"The devil has come to kill, steal, and destroy—I have come to give life abundantly." John 10:10

To choose to live forever (who wouldn't want that?), you simply take the blue pill—you choose to discard the lie (red pill and a false reality) and you give your life back to the creator and allow Him to be the one you follow with all your heart and mind. The devil is a liar and the father of lies. The greatest command is this:

You shall love the Lord your God with all your heart, soul, mind and strength, and the second is like it, and you shall love your neighbor as yourself.

Jesus warned us about this evil tyrant.

"The coming of the lawless one will be in accordance with how Satan works. He will use all sorts of displays of power through signs and wonders that serve the lie, and all the ways that wickedness deceives those who are perishing. They perish because they refused to love the truth and so be saved. For this reason God sends them a powerful delusion so that they will believe the lie and so that all will be condemned who have not believed the truth but have delighted in wickedness." 2 Thessalonians 2: 9-12 (NIV)

And:

"For this reason, God sends them something powerful that leads them away from the truth so they will believe a lie. So, all those will be judged guilty who did not believe the truth, but enjoyed doing evil." 2 Thessalonians 2:9-12 (NCV)

DAY 131

When it comes to spiritual growth, some people are looking for magic, and some for method.

The magic folks want hands laid on them so their character will change. They are looking for something that will happen instantly.

The ones looking for methods assume that safety is in structure: give me ten reasons, nine steps, six points; something I can organize my life with so I won't have to think, or be vulnerable so I can control my Christianity.

The truth is somewhere between those two extremes. Intimacy in relationship with God and vulnerability toward each other is the way to grow spiritually. If we really want to grow up, we must do the hard work of developing our relationship with God and His people.

A respected Christian leader once said: "too many people today focus on a cosmetic view of Christianity in which they see themselves in self-improvement programs. Come to Jesus and get your marriage fixed. Come to Jesus and become prosperous. Come to Jesus and get this or that blessing or thing. We emphasize strongly to come to Jesus because He is worthy to be worshipped—whether or not He fixes our marriages or heals our bodies or gives us new cars. We may go through life with a marriage partner who for one reason or another is never going to come to Christ or relate in a proper way, but Jesus is still worthy of our loyalty."

Spiritual growth has to be done intentionally, carefully and over time. It is like tending a garden: there are no short cuts. The weeds have to be pulled; there must be watering and sunshine and care for the soil. We tend, God grows; there is no other way.

DAY 132

When Leonardo de Vinci was forty-three years old, the Duke Ludovinco of Milan asked him to paint the dramatic scene of Jesus' last supper with His disciples.

Working slowly and giving meticulous care to details, he spent three years on the assignment. He grouped the disciples into threes, two groups on either side of the central figure of Christ. Christ's arms are outstretched. In His right hand, He holds a cup, painted beautifully with marvelous realism.

When the masterpiece was finished, the artist said to a friend, "Observe it and give me your opinion of it!"

"It's wonderful!" exclaimed the friend. "The cup is so real I cannot divert my eyes from it!"

Immediately Leonardo took a brush and drew it across the sparkling cup! He exclaimed as he did so: "Nothing shall detract from the figure of Christ!"

This may seem to a little harsh to us today, but that might tell us more about ourselves than Leonardo. Perhaps his passion for Jesus stands too starkly against our lukewarm indifference in the things of God that it causes us some shame. Perhaps that shame is both good and warranted in this case.

Becoming true worshippers is the chief assignment God has given us in this lifetime. God is bringing the church to her knees to teach her how to express in intimate, loving, adoring language, her love for Him and her appreciation of His blessing and care. In addition to what we often define as worship, the Lord calls us to live a life of worship. The Word, our walk with Jesus and the works of the church as a whole are all expressions of worship. They flow out of a heart that is devoted to worshipping Jesus.

DAY 133

W hen life hands you trouble, you need to dig. Dig below the surface of your experience. You need to dig below the surface of your expectations. You need to dig below the surface of your disappointments. You need to dig until you find the richness of faith.

It is like oil. Oil is precious to our way of life, but it is forged deep within the earth under tremendous pressure.

That is what we dig for; the kind of faith that is forged by the tremendous pressures of life. Don't give up. Don't give in. Don't settle for a shallow faith that puts on a plastic smile and says, "Everything is just fine".

That is what happened to Job. His wife looked at all his troubles and encouraged him to tell God where he could get off, and then die. His friends weren't much help either. They wanted to play the blame game. "All this suffering has to be somebody's fault" they reasoned. It must be you, Job.

But Job did not just lie there and take it. He dug deep. He told his friends, "I will never admit you are in the right; till I die, I will not deny my integrity. I will maintain my righteousness and never let go of it; my conscience will not reproach me as long as I live."

In the end, Job got his audience with God, and got put in his place. But he had gone deep and came out of it all with an unshaken, rich and noble faith. A faith that has been a bedrock of encouragement for thousands of years. So, the next time trouble hits, go deep and keep digging; and remember those, like Job, who have gone before us.

Then Job replied to the Lord : "I know that you can do all things; no plan of yours can be thwarted. You asked, 'Who is this that obscures my counsel without knowledge?' Surely I spoke of things I did not understand, things too wonderful for me to know. "You said, 'Listen now, and I will speak; I will question you, and you shall answer me.' My ears had heard of you but now my eyes have

seen you. Therefore I despise myself and repent in dust and
ashes." Job 42:1-6 NIV 84)

DAY 134

When we question God's actions or doubt His faithfulness, we are limited creatures trying to understand an infinite God. It is a dangerous game to create God in our own image, expecting Him to behave like us, judging Him by our standards, forcing upon Him our definitions of goodness, justice, and fairness. God is not a man or woman.

For many of us who have grown up in the church, we are taught, as early as Sunday School, how God works in the world. But we may begin to feel we have God figured out. We can become too familiar with God—we fail to embrace the paradox of the God who is both near and far.

God's ways are not our ways. We are locked into time and space. We live by the calendar, by our watches and our schedules. We have present, past and future. God has only the present; the eternal now.

How this plays out in our world is that God often takes longer than we expect. Abraham and Sarah experienced that, along with Moses, Hannah, and most of the prophets. God takes the long walk. For Him a thousand years are as a day and a day is as a thousand years. As one author put it: "With God, timing is more important than time."

God's value system is different from ours. For us the words "good" and "blessing" signify comfort and convenience and happy circumstances. But to God the same words may signify character and virtue and integrity. We think in physical and material terms; God thinks about the whole. To Him, holiness is better than happiness, character more desirable than comfort.

God has revealed Himself to us so that we might know Him and obey Him. He is not fond of standing under our microscopes as if we could understand Him that way. Attempts to understand God in order to figure Him out border on blasphemy and idolatry. He calls us to lay down even our understanding that we might know Him as He is, as He has revealed Himself to be to us.

"For my thoughts are not your thoughts, neither are your ways my ways," declares the LORD." Isaiah 55:8 (NIV)

DAY135

> "When we were utterly helpless, Christ came at just the right time and died for us sinners. Now, most people would not be willing to die for an upright person, though someone might perhaps be willing to die for a person who is especially good. But God showed His great love for us by sending Christ to die for us while we were still sinners." Romans 5:6-8 (NLT)

I f you were given an outrageous sum of money—say something like thirty million dollars, how would you spend it; some on friends and family, then some on yourself? Here is a question for you. How much would you spend on your enemies?

To say that Christ died for sinners means that God spent Jesus on those who were opposed to Him. Being a sinner means standing in the place of Adam and Eve, shaking our fist to God, saying "not your will, but our will be done." That's where we all were when Christ died for us. What incredible love, it blows your mind. We have a hard time just being nice to other Christians sometimes; how much less would we be willing to give up our very best for those who are against us. What love!

We have value not because of our accomplishments, not because of our potential, but because God has placed value upon us. What is the price of a human soul? What price has God paid? He has truly paid for us with His very own Son. There is no greater love than that.

Have you fully embraced the value God has placed on you—not because of what you've done, or what you may do, but because He has declared you valuable? Let me encourage you today. Give yourself fully to God and embrace the value He has placed on you.

DAY 136

While in London, evangelist D. L. Moody was approached by a man who wanted to know the secret of his success in evangelism. Moody directed the man to the hotel window and asked, "What do you see?" The man looked down and reported a view of the crowded streets. Moody suggested he look again. This time the man mentioned seeing people—men, women, and children. The man became frustrated as Moody directed him to look again. Moody joined him at the window with watery eyes and said, "I see people going to hell without Jesus. Until you see people like that, you will not lead them to Christ."

One night when Moody was going home, it occurred to him that he had not spoken to a single person that day about accepting Christ. A day lost, he thought to himself. But as he walked, he saw a man by a lamp post. He went up to him and asked, "are you a Christian?"

The next day a businessman friend sent for Moody. He told Moody that the stranger he had spoken to was a friend of his. "Moody...You've got zeal without knowledge. You insulted a friend of mine last night. You went up to him, a perfect stranger, and asked him if he were a Christian."

Moody went out of his friend's office heartbroken and for some time worried about this. Then late one night a man pounded on his door. It was the stranger he had supposedly insulted. The man said, "Mr. Moody, I have not had a good night's sleep since that night you spoke to me under the lamp post, and I have come around at this unearthly hour of the night for you to tell me what I have to do to be saved."

DAY 137

W hile you can work too much, it is not true that you can emphasize work too much. Work does not produce nervous breakdowns, despite what you may have been told. Work as hard as you like and as long as you like. If you're in normal health, you will come to little harm, especially if your labor is in the Lord.

Why? Because it is tension that kills, not work. It is getting caught in the Christian rat race that does the damage. It is the desperate fight to keep a front with Christian friends or with the Christian public. It is the desire to appear smilingly spiritual and produce spirituality when all the while your true inner life does not measure up to your exterior image.

Sometimes we work too much not because the work is essential, but because we are driven by fear rather than being sustained by faith. Workaholics are driven. Work for them is not an expression of faith, but a search for peace. Where some people seek to be justified by works, workaholics try to keep their consciences clean by working. Consequently, they work too much and become slaves to their own nervous activity. Workaholics cannot rest; they begin to look haunted when relaxing and turn every leisure activity into a new type of achievement that must be worked at and conquered.

God doesn't want us to be driven by anything. Life is a gift given to us and we are responsible to steward it the best we can. This is what Solomon said about life in Ecclesiastes 5:18:

"I have seen what is best for people here on earth. They should eat and drink and enjoy their work, because the life God has given them on earth is short." Amen.

DAY 138

"Who among you fears the Lord and obeys His servant? Let those who walk in darkness and have no light trust the name of the Lord and depend upon their God. But all of you light fires and arm yourselves with flaming torches. So walk in your own light and among the torches you have lit. This is what you will receive from me: You will be tormented." Isaiah 50:10-11 (GW)

I n his book, *The Heavenly Man*, brother Yun's wife Deling tells this story about being a young believer in China:

"At the age of eighteen I committed my life to Jesus Christ...Two other young women came to the Lord at the same time as me. We attended meetings together in different parts of the district, so we often had to walk more than an hour to get there. After the meetings I often walked home by myself. This was dangerous because it was so dark and there were evil men and wild dogs out late at night.

God worked a great miracle to protect and help me in those early days. Many nights as I walked home I could see a light about ten meters ahead of me on the path, showing me the way I needed to take. In the pitch dark I often lost my way, but then I'd see the light, like a small star, showing the way to get back on the right path. The light wasn't constant; it just appeared whenever I was heading in the wrong direction."

What a powerful testimony of God's miraculous provision. God is dependable—He might not always come through in the way we want or expect, but He is never far off; He is never absent.

We often, and will often, take wrong paths in our life. But if we will just hold on and not panic; if we will refuse to light our own fires in the darkness and chaos of our lives—and if we will just trust and depend on God, He will always guide us back to the right path.

DAY 139

"YOU MAY SAY TO YOURSELF, 'MY POWER AND THE STRENGTH OF MY HANDS HAVE PRODUCED THIS WEALTH FOR ME.' BUT REMEMBER THE LORD YOUR GOD, FOR IT IS HE WHO GIVES YOU THE ABILITY TO PRODUCE WEALTH." DEUTERONOMY 8:17-18 (NIV)

R emember. It is a theme that runs through the book of Deuteronomy. The children of Israel have been wandering around in the desert for forty years after failing to enter the Promised Land because of their unbelief. Now they are back where they started. Now they can take the land.

But Moses warns them. Remember. Remember all that God has done. Remember what God has said—His law, His commands. Remember what God has done—the deliverance from Egypt. Remember God's provision— the bread from Heaven, the clothes that did not wear out. Remember God's guidance—a pillar of fire by night and a cloud by day. Don't forget. When you finally settle down and life gets good and routine. When things become easier, don't forget.

We still need to heed this message. Many like to think of spiritual warfare as demons and angels battling it out in the heavenlies to the clanking of swords and crashing of shields, and sometimes it may look that way. Many see spiritual warfare in every difficult circumstance and every frustrated plan. But sometimes the warfare is more subtle and therefore more dangerous. Sometimes the enemy just wants to lure us into complacency. Sometimes the voice of the enemy is not so much a temptation to some hideous sin as much as it is a sing-song voice that lures us into forgetfulness. We forget God's faithfulness. We forget God's goodness. We forget God's provision. We forget that the life we have is not by our own making.

Remember the Lord your God.

DAY 140

Zephaniah 3:17 says, "The Lord your God is with you, He is mighty to save. He will take great delight in you, He will quiet you with His love, He will rejoice over you with singing."

In the Old Testament, God continually threatens punishment for those who don't follow His commands and incredible blessing for those who do. Within the scope of God's holiness and justice, He sometimes decrees genocide for godless nations—entire nations of peoples wiped out.

But you cannot escape God's wrath even in the New Testament. Jesus, who came as a servant and a sacrificial lamb, will return one day in judgment. The Scriptures talk of God's future judgment poured out on the earth in catastrophe, plague and natural disasters.

We don't understand. But then again, we underestimate the destructiveness and seriousness of sin. We want to put God on trial and determine if He's worth following. We want to question God as if we can be more loving and merciful than He.

But that's like trying to examine the Sun with a flashlight. All of our sense of justice, all of our understanding of love and mercy comes from Him alone. He is so vast that we cannot possibly take the small parts of Him that we think we understand and get a sense of everything that He is.

It is enough to know that He defines Himself as love. He doesn't say He has a lot of love. He defines His fundamental essence as love. It is who He is. God is love.

The word of the Lord that came to Zephaniah was that God takes delight in you. The Lord calms you with His love and dances over you with singing. Even now the Lord is dancing over you.

PRAYING AND MEDITATING ON THE SCRIPTURE

Learn how to use Scripture to grow in the knowledge and fullness of the Lord.

"'May the LORD bless you and keep you; may the LORD cause His face to shine upon you and be gracious to you; may the LORD lift up His countenance toward you and give you peace.'" Numbers 6:24-26

M oses used the whole book of Deuteronomy to strengthen the people in the Lord by repeating and restating things they should have known. The Lord commanded the people, through Moses, to meditate on what God had taught them and to even teach it to their children.

"These commandments that I give you today are to be upon your hearts. Impress them on your children. Talk about them when you sit at home and when you walk along the road, when you lie down and when you get up. Tie them as symbols on your hands and bind them on your foreheads. Write them on the doorframes of your houses and on your gates." Deuteronomy 6:6-9 (NIV)

There were worship leaders in the Tabernacle of David who were selected to minister in song and word. They had to be at least thirty years of age and well versed in the Scripture. They were praying and declaring Scripture, reminding the people of His promises, like in Psalm 105:8-9:

"He remembers His covenant forever, the word He commanded, for a thousand generations, the covenant He made with Abraham, the oath He swore to Isaac."

You might have noticed the word selah in the Psalms. The exact meaning of "Selah" in the Bible is uncertain, but it is believed to be a musical term indicating a pause or reflection and is thought to guide musical direction or prompt contemplation on the text. This word carries the idea to meditate on a passage and apply it to your life.

Now we will take a look at some Bible passages in which the Holy Spirit, speaking through His people, instructs us what exactly God wants us to declare.

"But you are a chosen race, a royal priesthood, a holy nation, a people of His own, so that you may proclaim the virtues of the One who called you out of darkness into His marvelous light." 1 Peter 2:9 (NIV)

"Pray for me also, that I may be given the message when I begin to speak - that I may confidently make known the mystery of the gospel, for which I am an ambassador in chains. Pray that I may be able to speak boldly as I ought to speak." Ephesians 6:19 (NIV)

"Declare His glory among the nations, His wonders among all peoples." 1 Chronicles 16:24 & Psalm 96:3 (NIV)

"O Lord, see how my enemies persecute me! Have mercy and lift me up from the gates of death, that I may declare Your praises in the gates of the Daughter of Zion and there rejoice in Your salvation." Psalm 9:13-14 (NIV)

"I will declare your [Yahweh's] name to my countrymen! In the middle of the assembly, I will praise you!" Psalm 22:22 (NIV)

"O Lord, open my lips, that my mouth may declare Your praise." Psalm 51:15 (NIV)

"O God, You have taught me since I was young, and I am still declaring Your amazing deeds." Psalm 71:17 (NET)

"Now also when I am old and gray-headed, O God, do not forsake me, until I declare Your strength to this generation, Your power to everyone who is to come." Psalm 71:18 (NKJV)

"I declare that Your steadfast love is established forever; Your faithfulness is as firm as the heavens." Psalm 89:2 (NRSV)

Declaring His truth over us about who He says He is activates our faith and connects those truths with our spirits.

As we declare this truth, He is aligning our thoughts and feelings and attitudes with God's truth about His nature and our nature in Christ. It is resetting our true north. That alignment is like the renewing of our minds in Romans 12:2; as we meditate on and declare the truth of God's Word, our minds become renewed.

We know that the early church prayed back to God the very words that God had given them.

We see this in Acts 4:24 and following; in fact, they explicitly quote Scriptures. Threats had been made against them and it says,

---

"They lifted their voices together to God and said, 'Sovereign Lord, who made the Heaven and the earth and the sea and everything in them."

They are exulting in what they know is from God in Scripture.

Then verses 25–26 say:

"Who through the mouth of our father David, Your servant, said by the Holy Spirit, 'Why did the Gentiles rage, and the peoples plot in vain? The kings of the earth set themselves, and the rulers were gathered together, against the Lord and against His anointed'"

That is a quotation from Psalm 2.

Don't forget the obvious; namely, that many parts of the Scripture are prayers. So, simply reading much of them is to pray, if we are awake — that is, if we are thinking about what we are doing. Paul has got numerous prayers that he prays for the people that he is writing his letters to. And every time we read those kinds of prayers we should pray with Paul. And a great portion of the Psalms are prayers, as are many of Jesus words.

So, the Scripture models for us how to read the Scriptures and turn them into prayers.

The Scriptures either tell us something about God and Christ when we are reading in order to praise Him, or they tell us something about what God and Christ and the Holy Spirit have done so that we can thank Him and express faith in it. Or they tell us what God expects from us so that we can cry out for his help. They tell us who we are in Him and boosts our confidence in the Lord. Or, they tell us about something we failed to do so that we can confess our sins.

Here is a simple prayer to practice praying the scripture based on the 23rd Psalm:

"Lord, I thank you that you are my shepherd, that you watch over me and keep me and in you I have all I need. I am grateful how, especially in the busyness of life, you make me lie down in green pastures in peace; you lead me beside sill waters and you heal my soul, refreshing and cleansing me. Thank you for leading me to live rightly so that I don't defame your wonderful Name. And Lord I know, that even as I walk through tough times of despair and it seems like I may not make it, I won't let fear live rent free in my head. My hope is always in your salvation. I will live as long as you have ordained for me to live. I praise you and thank you! Your rod for correction and your staff for protection. You are the Good Shepherd. I know that life is not always fair, and my enemies sometimes triumph over me. But in the midst of it all, you prepare a feast for me right in the midst of them. I am anointed with the oil of your presence and it just runs all over me, blessing me, purifying me, honoring me. Goodness and mercy follow along behind me because of your goodness— they are constantly in my mirror no matter what is going on in my circumstances. And the end! In the end I get to live in your big old house with you forever. You bless me Lord. Thank you! Amen."

The Bible is far more than mere information—it is divine revelation. Its five core themes—God's nature, His deeds, His expectations, our identity, and our sins—are truths we could not grasp without divine disclosure. As the living Word of God, it is vibrant, active, and sharper than any two-edged sword. Reading it with humility and a hunger to know God immerses us in a supernatural realm of wonder and awe. It fosters intimate knowledge of Him, not just facts about Him. The Bible is inherently formative, even transformative, a living map pointing us our True North, the Morning Star, the beloved Son, Jesus. Stay aligned! Stay anchored! Stay true!

"May the Lord bless you and protect you; may the Lord make his face shine on you and be gracious to you; may the Lord look with favor on you and give you peace." Numbers 6:24-26 (NLT)